Camping in
High Heels

Camping in High Heels

MIKI BENNETT

This book is a work of fiction. Any references to historical events, real people, or real places are used fictitiously. Other names, characters, places, and events are products of the author's imagination, and any resemblance to actual events or places or persons, living or dead, is entirely coincidence.

Cover image by Donna Lee Gauntlett

ISBN: 0692752226
ISBN 13: 9780692752227
Library of Congress Control Number: 2016911304
WannaDo Concepts Publishing, Charleston, SC

This book is dedicated to my loving parents, Sonny and Irene. Your forty-five years in the recreational vehicle industry have given me such wonderful memories to turn into fun stories about camping. I love you both!

"It's okay to be a newbie to the camping world. You will get the hang of it," Brandon said, and he fell in step beside her.

"Why does everyone keep saying that? I feel as if I'm on display or something." Kate was feeling embarrassed once more.

"Hey, at some point, all of us were in your shoes. Well, maybe not your high heels."

Kate felt the color drain from her face. He had to have seen her wobbly, awkward walk to her camper last night. "What are you talking about?" she said, feigning innocence.

"Last night I thought you were pretty drunk till I saw you all dressed up with those heels on. It's a wonder you didn't break your ankle the way you were walking last night. You must have hit every piece of gravel on the road." Brandon chuckled once more, and Kate blushed as they continued their walk toward the store.

"No, I wasn't drunk. But why were you spying on me?"

"I wasn't spying on you. I was sitting outside and enjoying the evening. You just happened to walk by. That is to say, wobble by."

"Do you enjoy making fun of people?" Kate said. She wanted to be irritated at his remark but found it hard to keep the feeling each time she glanced in his direction.

"You're right. I'll stop. But watching you walk to your camper last night was the highlight of my evening."

One

*W*hat had she been thinking! As she drove through the campground, Kate Palmer quickly spotted her site for the evening: #30. I wonder if that means something, she thought, as she rolled her eyes. Given she was thirty-years old and she was on her first ever camping experience, she figured this must be a sign from above. She wondered if it was meant for her to take this miserable trip—whether she liked it or not.

This wasn't the first time she had traveled on her own, that was for sure. But this was the first day of her trip around the United States by herself, and it was in a motor home! According to her thousands of avid blog readers, though, she was cheating just a bit. Since Kate had been given the use of an RV, many people said she had it too easy.

"Easy! Ugh!" Kate shouted out loud to herself.

There was definitely nothing easy about parking a house with wheels in a space she was sure was designed for one of those Mini Cooper cars! All the practice in the world on how to use her rolling home still had not prepared her for the "simple" task before her. She had to park Monster, as she had so lovingly nicknamed her twenty-five-foot motor coach, in the camp space in front of her, and this wasn't even the first endeavour of the day that had thrown her completely out of her comfort zone.

From the time Kate left the security of the dealership near Spartanburg, South Carolina, she had already experienced quite a few things that had her nerves so frazzled she was about to bite her beautiful nails down to their quicks. That would definitely ruin the nice manicure Kate had treated herself to just a few days before beginning her momentous adventure. The bright pink color made her smile but also helped her keep her pretty nails away from her teeth all day. Instead of biting her fingernails, Kate had talked to people in cars and trucks—even though they couldn't hear her. It seemed to her they always got too close, and she would cringe inside. They would also honk their horns if she was not moving fast enough or, in one instance, going the wrong way! And this was just day one.

To add insult to injury, Kate had planned for her first day to be such a breeze that she could travel from South Carolina to the Gulf Coast, staying in Biloxi, Mississippi. The drive was only a little over eight hours, so leaving at seven o'clock in the morning was supposed to give her a nice late-afternoon arrival. She figured she'd have the evening to relax and maybe time to do some work at her first campground. Little did she know that her trip would turn into an eleven-hour ordeal. By the time she drove through the entrance where she was to stay for two nights, Kate was whipped. *Where are my bathrobe and slippers? And I would love some room service right now,* Kate thought. She was still staring at the tiny parking spot before her. If she could just get this thing in position, she could breathe a short sigh of relief and sit still for a moment.

On the day Kate decided that college wasn't for her, she had no idea that one day she would be a world traveler, being paid to take wondrous trips and write about her incredible experiences. She had never received more than a B in English in either high school or college, so writing as a career had never even been a thought. Kate had tried many jobs, and then one day, standing in line for her daily latte, she struck up a conversation with the woman behind her. Kate found out she was a travel agent, and the more they talked, the more Kate was intrigued. She learned all she could about becoming an agent herself and finally convinced a local agency to hire her solely on commission. With Kate's determination and all her previous contacts, her travel sales soared and made her the top agent in a very short time. Soon she was traveling free all over the world, earning trips for her high sales numbers.

When Kate decided to write a blog about her experiences, it was no more than just a hobby. She actually thought of it as a daily journal of sorts. But before she knew it, her readership grew to the point that companies started contacting her to advertise on her blog, *Watch Kate Travel*. It became a second source of income, a very profitable one at that, plus she was doing something she completely loved—traveling to some of the most sought after destinations around the world and mostly for free. She gave her devoted readers travel tips, told them about places to see, and things to try at beautiful places all over the world. At her age, Kate felt as if she had it made. She was living a jet-setting life out of two suitcases and a carry-on, and she always had her trusty laptop with her. But she never thought her extremely popular blog would lead to a six-month trip around the United States in a motor home.

All it took for the change in her travel style, though, was a comment from one of her many loyal readers: Bubba. He was sweet, but this one statement changed her world: "You like traveling to all these fancy places, flying first class and staying in five-star hotels. But what about those of us who can't come and go like that? Why don't you try something simpler like camping? You would get to see some great places. Bet you can't do it." That was it. That one little comment on her blog had caused an uproar like nothing she had ever experienced since starting her website. Everyone was excited to see if Kate would take on the challenge. There were more replies to Bubba's comment than any other before, and soon her social media visitors were wondering and asking the same question: Would the pampered traveler take the camping plunge?

I have to make this work, Kate thought. She was still looking at her camp space as though it was challenging her to a duel. She carefully inched into the site, stopping and starting so much that she kept her fingers crossed the brakes wouldn't burn out. Plus, she could hear everything she had so neatly packed in the camper shuffling around with each start and stop. Kate looked in the side mirror to see if she was lined up with those things she had to connect to the motor home, and she couldn't figure out if she was or not. She carefully put the vehicle in park, got out to check, and was so proud. She had matched them up perfectly. Then a frown crossed her face as she realized she was going to have to hook up the water, electric cord and the dreaded sewer hose. Ugh!

When the people at the dealership had explained everything she would need to do to hook the motor home up at each campground, Kate had smiled sweetly while cringing on the inside. Everything was OK until she found out about the sewer hose. Just the thought had grossed her out! But she was prepared.

Kate walked around and jumped back into the driver's seat, turning off the motor. She had finally made her way completely onto the site, and she smiled at her accomplishment. I did it, Kate thought. A huge grin was on her face, and sweat was running down her forehead. Even though it had been a very long first day, she had arrived in Biloxi, Mississippi. She was officially on the road. Take that, Bubba, Kate thought, and she stepped outside the motor home and looked around. Now, she just had to remember all those things she had to do in order to have some luxuries while on this trip of hers.

The RV dealership in Spartanburg, South Carolina, had been so gracious to let her use a motor home for her journey, but this had taken away any chance to gracefully back out of the trip. A motor home for six months of travel around the United States. Oh yeah, Kate thought weakly the day they contacted her.

Then when she arrived to pick up the RV, they had shown her how everything worked in the rolling house. Kate even recorded each thing the young man showed her about how all the little doodads worked because there was no way she was going to remember everything. She felt a little panicky at the thought of making sure everything was correctly set up at the campgrounds she would visit, but at least it was on video. This helped her feel just a tiny bit more confident but not much. The dealership was excited to be part of her journey. The young man told her he would be following her on Facebook, and he said he couldn't wait to see where she was going. Who doesn't know about this fiasco? Kate thought. This has really turned into a media circus.

As Kate took a minute to sit at the picnic table, she thought about what she had left behind at home. Usually her trips were one or two weeks. This adventure was altogether different, though. Kate had been sure her father would have some words of wisdom to help her back out gracefully from this venture, but from the moment Kate told him all about it, Martin Palmer had been all for it. He even said that if he hadn't had to work, he would have loved to come along! He kept telling Kate about all the wonderful places she could visit, and the two of them even sat down and made a tentative itinerary for her to follow, but her father had made her promise to be flexible. He wanted his little girl to see as much of the United States as she could during this once-in-a-lifetime gift.

Then there was Thomas. They had been dating for a little while, but they both knew it was more of a friendship than a romantic relationship. The moment she told him about the trip, Thomas sat quietly and didn't say a word. Almost simultaneously, they said the same thing: I don't think this is going to work between us. The words came out so quickly that they both laughed. Even though Kate was worried about the trip, it had helped her and Thomas realize they were just good friends. That was all. Thomas did encourage her to go and to see everything she could. Kate had been almost certain he would have advised her not to go. It made her wonder why everyone was so excited about this trip except her?

As she finally got up from her place at the picnic table, it was time for the thing she truly dreaded: making sure she had electricity and water. Oh, and that nasty sewer hose. Kate opened up the side compartment that held what she needed to put her rolling house back on the grid, so to speak. The water hose she remembered how to do, and it was attached in no time. The electric cord was another check off the list. So far, so good. Now, however, she was glad she had tucked disposable gloves and a bottle of hand sanitizer in the same compartment. After the gloves were on, Kate removed the never-used sewer hose and the notes she had neatly typed and laminated from their hiding place. After reading the instructions at least three times, she placed the hose into the nasty little hole in the ground. It had a slightly pungent odor, and caused Kate to wrinkle her nose and squint her eyes. Next she attached the other end of the hose to the motor home, and she double-checked that all valves for the water and sewer were in their correct positions. This was crucial because she had been given an ominous warning. Pull the wrong lever at the wrong time, and she could end up with dirty water and sewage all over. She read every step on her little sheet of paper, though, and before she knew it, she was hooked up. Kate stood quickly and gave a loud, "Woo-Hoo!" Then she looked around to see if anyone was watching. If people had been observing her, they would have known immediately she was a newbie to this camping thing.

As Kate walked back to the motor home entrance, she remembered she could put that thing out to cover her little patio. What was it called? She tried to recall what the young man at the dealership had called it but couldn't remember. It didn't matter.

Just getting parked and hooking up the necessities was enough for her. Besides, she would only be here for a few nights before heading to New Orleans. Her readers had made so many suggestions of places to visit that she could have stayed on the road for over a year! Right now, she only looked forward to two places on her planned itinerary: her next stop and one place she actually was excited to see, the Grand Canyon.

As Kate looked around her, she wondered why anyone would want to do this. Why do all this work when you can have a nice hotel with a soft bed, room service anytime, and a taxi or limo to take you places? If not for Bubba and his innocent comment, she would have been on a plane to London right now, a wonderful trip she had been offered at the last minute but had to turn down because of her sudden camping quest. Six months of this!

As she glanced around the campground, though, there was a feeling in the air she couldn't quite describe. Peaceful? No way! Not after all the driving, parking, and setting up. Pretty? Yes, the campground was nice. She could even see the beach from where she was parked though it was a small distance away. It still wasn't that, though. Hopefully she would figure out what she was trying to describe—this feeling that just wouldn't go away as she looked around at the various campers and people surrounding her.

Though she was tired, Kate decided to take a small walk around the place. She wanted to see what all the fuss was about. She had done research—lots of it—before agreeing to this experiment and found that a large segment of the US population loved to get out in the great outdoors, whether it was camping, hiking, backpacking, or more. She found that fact interesting, but she loved her manicure and pedicure dates, the complimentary massages at those classy hotels, and limos that would take her to and from her desired destinations. She loved the parties, the fashion, and everything that had become her world these last few years. As she looked around the campground, she had never felt so out of place and was already homesick for Charleston.

As Kate continued her stroll, she saw all types of people: families, retired couples, and even those traveling by themselves. The variety of vehicles seemed almost endless. She saw everything from tents to bus-size motor homes, which Kate had always assumed were only for celebrities. One vehicle in particular intrigued her the most. It was a vintage Volkswagen van with a little tent pitched beside it. It looked as though it was right out of the sixties, and it was restored beautifully. She loved those old vans and had secretly always wanted one. It seemed in excellent condition. She had never imagined a vehicle like that for camping. She took a quick picture with her iPhone and considered using it when she wrote her blog tonight. This will definitely be an interesting picture for Instagram and Facebook, she thought. That reminded her. She had to take a picture with her selfie stick by the motor home and make sure the dealership received a picture of her with their camper, proving that, at least for this first day, they were both still intact.

"Is your name Kate?" came a voice from someone who was suddenly standing in front of her.

She looked to see an older woman staring up at her while holding a leash to a little dog sitting on the ground next to it's owners feet. Kate was a little disconcerted. How did this woman know her name? "I am. How are you? And how do you know me?" Kate was making an effort to be polite while still trying to figure out how the woman knew her.

"From your blog."

"You recognized me from my blog?"

"Of course. Best travel info as far as I'm concerned. Been reading it for quite some time now. By the way, loved your tips for Hong Kong. They were spot on when Henry and I visited last year." The little lady continued to stare at Kate as if she was some kind of celebrity. "Henry!" the woman yelled suddenly. "Come here! This here is that girl I was telling you about. You know? The one who writes on the computer. She really is going on that camping trip!" She quickly turned her attention back to Kate. "Personally, I didn't think you would do it. I thought maybe it was one of those things y'all do to get attention. Sorry! But you are really here, and this is your first day, right?"

"Uh...yes," Kate said. She was still doing her best to digest everything that was happening before her.

"Hello, young lady," said the man Kate supposed was Henry. He walked up and extended his hand.

"Hi." It was the only word to come out of Kate's mouth.

She really didn't know what to say because it instantly hit her that she usually only talked to her readers through her blog, social media accounts, and occasional interviews. When she traveled, Kate would talk to the locals to make sure she got some great information to share with her readers, but it was never anyone who knew who she was. Kate and the couple continued to stare at each other, Kate shifting from one foot to the other while wringing her hands in nervousness. What do I say now, she thought.

"I'm not on the computer much. That's Jean's thing, but she has talked about you quite a lot—especially lately. I have to admit, your advice has made a lot of our trips enjoyable. Thought you were one of those fancy girls, though. Are you staying here in the campground?" Henry asked, and he looked puzzled.

Jean gave her husband a small punch in the arm. "Remember? I told you about her and the camping trip. She is traveling the United States for a while in a motor home. Someone even gave her one to use. Don't you remember anything I tell you?" Jean said to her husband, a little aggravated and she rolled her eyes.

Kate didn't want the couple to break into an argument, so she kindly butted in. "Yes, I'm actually right over there. Spot number thirty," she said and pointed to her motor home.

"Looks as if you've got yourself a really nice coach there. We are over there in that travel trailer." Henry pointed to a rather large trailer with a nice truck parked beside it.

"Why don't you join us for dinner tonight?" Jean said, and she looked up at Kate with expectant eyes while nodding her head. "We're fixing burgers on the grill, Henry's specialty when we're camping."

Kate's immediate response was going to be no, but as she looked at Jean, she couldn't find a way to gracefully bow out of the invitation. This sweet lady was one of her actual readers and she was also so friendly. Kate didn't have the heart to tell her she usually didn't eat hamburgers. She knew that would sound a bit snobbish. She had already planned to fix something quick in her microwave—if she could figure out how to operate the appliance. Then it was off to work on her blog article. Once she reached New Orleans, she figured she would be able to get some decent food.

"I won't take no for an answer. We eat in about thirty minutes. Remember, we are right over there!" Jean said excitedly and turned around quickly. She walked so fast to her camper with her little dog almost running to keep up.

As Kate stood there, all she could think about was how she just wanted to eat and go to bed. The day had been quite hectic and very long. Even though she suddenly had instant friends on her first day, the homesickness she felt earlier still was lingering. She felt she couldn't do this trip at all and just wanted to go back home. OK, Kate. Put your big-girl panties on, and pull yourself together, she said to herself sternly. She took a deep breath and headed to her camper to get dressed for dinner with her new campground buddies, Henry and Jean.

Two

$\mathcal{H}$er first dinner out on the road was much better than she had expected. Kate's hosts had not only invited her but their neighbors on either side of their camp spot. They were all older than Kate, but she remained the center of attention—especially once Jean told them her story. Every person seated around the small campfire asked her questions.

"How do you blog?"

"What was your best trip ever?"

"What places are you planning to see on your camping trip?"

Kate could barely eat with all the questions being tossed at her so fast. Since she was considered a novice in the camping world, everyone then bombarded her with so many tips and tricks about dealing with RVs that she couldn't even remember the first one. Her biggest shock, though, was when everyone wanted pictures with her! Kate was being treated like a celebrity, and it felt weird, but she had to admit she liked it too. Right now, though, she was just plain tired and so ready to go to bed for her first night in the motor home.

Also, during dinner, Kate had a full view of the Volkswagen van she had seen earlier and was able to see more details of the tent pitched beside it. Of all the vehicles in the campground, it was the most unusual, and Kate was in love with it. What really caught her attention, though, was the man who emerged from the tent.

He seemed at least six feet tall, if not a few inches more. Even though Kate couldn't make out all his features, she could tell he would grab any woman's attention. He wore a white tank top that clearly showed the very defined musculature of his arms and a pair of loose shorts that gave Kate a nice view of tanned, muscular legs. His dark hair had a slight curl to it and gave him that beach surfer look. He looked more like a male model than someone camping in a tent. The mystery man grabbed a small tote bag, threw a towel over his shoulder, and then started walking up the little driveway—but not before looking her way. They made eye contact only for a second and that was all, but Kate couldn't help but watch him as he walked up the road till he was out of sight.

That was when she remembered what the young girl had told her at check-in. They had a bathhouse—the building where their campers could take showers. This completely grossed out Kate. The mere thought of taking a shower in a room with a bunch of strangers made her shudder. It brought back horrible flashbacks from high school gym class. She had already made up her mind that these bathhouses were strictly off limits during her trip! Besides showering with people she didn't know, she could just imagine the bugs that would probably be in the nasty bathrooms. Plus there was no telling what kind of perverts would linger around the building. The only shower her feet would touch was the one in the motor home or the occasional hotel she had promised herself as treats on this trip. Right now, though, she continued to stare up the road where the handsome man had disappeared.

"So?" Jean asked.

Kate suddenly looked back to her dinner guests, seeing all eyes were on her. "I'm sorry. What did you say?"

"What's your next stop, or is it a secret?" Jean said quickly.

"I'm heading toward New Orleans but keeping my options open. That way I can write about the activities I planned for and the things I just happen to find along the way. Like tonight. Everyone here has made my first day of camping really special." She hadn't realized that she had drifted away from the conversation, so taken by the man walking down the gravel road.

As she said her good-byes, Jean came over and pulled Kate to the side. "Sweetheart, it has been such a pleasure having you at dinner tonight. We are leaving tomorrow sometime, but if you should need anything before then, just let us know. Just a bit of womanly advice, though. You might want to think about wearing something a bit more casual for a dinner around a campfire. Don't get me wrong! Your outfit is too cute, but you might want to save those clothes for when you are in those big cities. Maybe going out to a fancy restaurant or something. You have a nice evening." Jean smiled, gave her a quick hug and turned around to head back to the small group.

As soon as Kate got in her motor home, she went straight to the long mirror on the closet door and looked at her clothes. She thought she had picked out an outfit that was totally appropriate for dinner: a pair of dark-brown skinny jeans, a tucked-in blouse that had a peasant neckline dotted with just a few sequins for sparkle, dangle earrings, and brown strappy sandals with a slight heel. Then she remembered the other guests and realized she probably had overdressed just a bit. Even Jean had only been dressed in a white tee shirt, jean shorts and a pair of old flip-flops. But what Kate had worn to dinner was the only type of clothes she had brought on her trip. This was what she considered "casual" when she wasn't dressed up. So it seemed that maybe a shopping trip would be in order tomorrow. When getting ready for this camping trip, she really hadn't thought about what she would be wearing. She now began a shopping list in her head: jeans, casual shirts, sneakers, and maybe some flip-flops. These all seemed more appropriate for her camping adventure but totally different than what Kate was used to.

As soon as she was in her camper, Kate bathed in her tiny shower, feeling like she was in a phone booth. There was barely room for her shampoo, conditioner, and soap, but she made it through. As she dried off, she kept thinking about her hotel treats that would be coming up—when she could have a luxurious bath along with a robe and slippers. She also couldn't help but think about her evening she had just experienced.

Everyone had seemed so friendly tonight. The campground had a relaxed vibe that she had never encountered before during her travels. Granted, a five-star hotel could have a peaceful feeling, but this was different. What perplexed her was she couldn't quite put it into words—at least not yet. There was no rushing to get from point *A* to point *B* and Kate realized something else. Once she had set up the outside hookups for the camper, even though it still made her feel squeamish, the quietness of the RV felt nice.

Since she had already made up the bed in the back of the motor home before leaving for her trip, Kate was able to quickly crawl between the sheets with her laptop. She opted tonight not to turn on the flat-screen television in the wall. It felt strange at first because she always went to bed with the television blaring every night, but this evening was different.

She opened up her laptop and began writing her first blog post about her trip. As Kate typed the words, she couldn't believe all the experiences she already had to draw from. In just one day, she had been through and accomplished so much. She had met such friendly people, drove an actual RV, parked it successfully, and spotted a very nice-looking guy. "Mr. VW Van" was pretty hunky but also a mystery man. That was also how he would probably remain since she was on the go. It seemed as if her trip would be a solo one, and Kate felt in her heart that this was OK. Honestly, a romantic relationship while on this trip would only complicate things. And if she was honest with herself, it felt kind of good to have this time just for herself.

The next morning, Kate woke to the smell of bacon wafting into her little camper. She didn't know where it was coming from, but the smell was so enticing and a wonderful way to wake up. She was still snuggled under the warmth of the blankets. It had been just a little chilly last night, and she didn't want to get up, but the aroma of breakfast foods cooking somewhere nearby had her fully alert now.

As she sat in bed and looked around her little sleeping space, Kate all at once realized she had slept the whole night. Usually she was up at least once a night with thoughts and ideas always swirling around in her head, but last night had been different. She felt rested, even though yesterday had been a bit of a challenge. Kate looked at the clock, and it read 7:10 a.m. and she was shocked. She was always up at six o'clock every morning—even without an alarm clock. She quickly jumped out of bed, put the sheets and blankets back into place and started to get dressed. She didn't dress to go to work, though. No, she was on a mission to find the source of the wonderful breakfast food smells coming from outside.

As she quickly raced around the motor home, Kate stopped. Why was she in such a hurry? She wasn't on a timetable, for once in a very long time. She had to admit that was one thing she had looked forward to about this trip when she was listing the pros and cons to decide whether to accept the challenge of this venture. No rushing to meet a plane, a dinner meeting, and more. She could actually take her time, plan things, or just go with the flow.

Anyway, just where was she heading today? Biloxi was known for its casinos, beaches, and more, but she did need to buy some clothes, so shopping it was. Then she wanted to enjoy some of the white sandy beaches not far from the campground. Her only problem would be transportation, but she could always call a taxi. She was a pro at that. Maybe that evening she would take a trip to the casino, even though she wasn't much of a gambler. This would give her more information for her blog, though, and show her readers she was enjoying something about the city where she was staying. Her next stop would be New Orleans. Kate knew she wanted to stay there for a couple of days, but hadn't her readers wanted her to try new experiences and smaller towns as she traveled from place to place—not the bigger cities?

As Kate thought about it some more, it was really that her readers wanted her to challenge herself to do something out of her comfort zone. They also wanted her to do activities that possibly everyone could do one day, traveling across America or just seeing the amazing places close to where they lived. Tomorrow she would leave for New Orleans where she already had a dinner scheduled with an old friend. She even had plans to try something new in the city—a tourist attraction she never had an interest in but one suggested by her blog readers. It was something she had never done on her many trips to the Big Easy. As for a place to stay, Kate already had a reservation at a campground near the city, so she could use a taxi to visit her friend and sightsee around town.

Kate had to will herself to slow down and enjoy the morning. She got dressed as slowly as she could, but for some reason, it was taking all her willpower not to move at her usual lightning speed. Am I always doing things in such a hurry? she quickly thought. Like my life is on high-speed mode?

As she stepped outside, the breakfast smells that had filled her motor home earlier now became more potent. While glancing around the campground, she could see many people fixing their breakfasts outside on grills. Kate had never experienced anything like this, and she could feel a smile spreading across her face. There was a very slight chill in the air, and she pulled her thin sweater around her as she walked to the camp store to see if there was any coffee to be found. Unfortunately, she had forgotten to put some in her motor home before she left on her trip. She could remedy this today when she went shopping.

As she made her way to the camp store, Kate couldn't help but check out the space where the good-looking mystery man in the VW van was parked. She was secretly hoping to get a glimpse of him once again—especially now that it was full daylight. He was still there, but she didn't see any movement around his site. Maybe he has left for the day, Kate thought. She felt a little disappointment that she hadn't been able to see him. Ugh! This was only her second day on the road, and she was looking for some hunky guy. This was a working camping trip, she reminded herself. Nothing more. Still, she couldn't help but think about the man she had seen last night.

"Hi, Jean," Kate said as she saw her new friend walking in the same direction as her.

"Good morning," she said, and she came up beside Kate quickly. "So, what do you have planned for today—if I may be so nosy?"

"Coffee first. Hopefully they will have some up here at the store. Then I'm going to catch a taxi to do a bit of shopping. I want to thank you for your advice. My clothing wasn't very casual last night. I'm not used to being able to wear something that wouldn't be deemed proper for work and I looked last night to find I don't really have a lot of casual clothing. But after I shop, then I thought I would check out the beach and kinda just go from there. Are you guys getting ready to leave?" Kate asked.

"We are in just a bit, but why don't you let us take you to the shopping center? That way you don't have to call a taxi."

"I'll probably be a while."

"Then at least let us drop you off," the older lady said with a big smile on her face.

Kate looked at her and thought she had to be the nicest person ever. "I think I'll take you up on that offer," Kate said.

She opened the door to the store, but she didn't have to put any strength behind the attempt. The door swung wide open very quickly, hitting her in the head! Three kids scurried out really fast, chatting nonstop and totally oblivious that they had just about knocked her out.

"Are you OK?" a male voice said.

Kate looked up to see it was him. The guy in the VW van. Up close, he was even more handsome—so much so that the words she wanted to say wouldn't come out.

"Do you have a cut? Seemed as if that door hit you pretty hard," the man said.

"I think I'm fine. I've got a pretty hard head." Kate tried to laugh, but then she realized the site was pretty sore.

"I think she'll be fine," Jean said to the stranger. "We will keep an eye on her. Have a nice day." With that, she ushered Kate into the store. "Whew, you have to watch out for men like that out on the road. No telling what he wanted," Jean said in a defensive voice.

Kate wanted to laugh. "Jean, he was just making sure I was OK. He didn't do anything wrong," Kate said. In a way, she wished Jean hadn't been there. She was sure she would have been able to talk to the very attractive man who had definitely caught her eye.

"Well, you be careful. There are a lot of those weirdos out there, you know what I mean? Campgrounds are some of the safest places, but you just never know these days."

"I promise I will stay on the lookout for these dangerous men," Kate said, giving her a wink.

"Just trying to take care of you. Then again, you have been all over the world, huh?"

"Yes, but thank you for being so caring," Kate said, and she smiled kindly at the protective woman by her side.

Pretty soon, Henry and Jean dropped her off at the Edgewater Mall, but this was not before they took one more picture together and made promises to keep in touch through e-mail on the blog. Then Kate found the necessary stores to take her wardrobe down a few notches. The more clothes she tried on, though, the more she liked them. The jeans, shorts, sneakers, casual shirts, and flip-flops felt so easy and free compared to her usual clothing. She actually couldn't wait to get back to the campground and wash them.

Before she made her way to the Laundromat with her new clothes, Kate walked to the beach across the street and just lay in the sun, soaking up the sunshine and watching all the people go by. By the time she was ready to head back, she had sand everywhere, but she didn't care. Kate couldn't remember the last time she had just sat at the beach with no agenda. It was only day two, and she could feel, just slightly, that she was beginning to relax.

By the time she got back to the camper and washed her clothes and herself, it was time for dinner. Kate grabbed a few things from the refrigerator and used the microwave to fix her something to eat. She smiled to herself as she took it outside to eat at her picnic table. She had actually figured out how to use something on her own. Granted, it was only a microwave, but it was a microwave in an RV. That was a victory in her book—even if it was one she would keep to herself. Before bed, she called her dad, and they talked awhile. Kate told him about her quasi celebrity status. He just wanted to make sure she was OK driving the big rig and was staying safe. Kate could hear the worry in his voice, but she reassured him she was OK. She also told him she wished he was there with her.

The next morning, Kate made sure everything was secure inside the motor home as much as she could. Then it was time to unhook everything outside. Once again, the thought made Kate cringe, but she dutifully went outside, donned her disposable gloves, and followed the laminated checklist sheet to the letter. Before long, she was ready to head to her next stop—New Orleans.

As she drove her camper very carefully out of the driveway, she slowed down just enough to check to see if the VW van and tent were still there. She just wanted one more look at this handsome man. As she drove by, the campsite was empty. He was already gone.

Three

Since Kate was so close to the next stop on her trip, she decided to take her rolling home down Highway 90, which took her along the Gulf Coast. It was beautiful, and she loved the scenery. Whenever she could, she stopped along the way and took picture after picture. These would be great proof of her journey for the blog. Kate couldn't get over the splendor of this place. Her dinner mates the other night had suggested this route, and since she had never seen Lake Pontchartrain, she decided to cut over to I-10 and then to I-12. Then she took the exit that led her over the beautiful estuary. It was the world's longest bridge—nearly forty miles—over a body of water that was so vast. As she began her drive across the long bridge, she snapped pictures in each direction. She was not sure what would show up on her camera, but she was careful to watch the road before her. This was only her second day officially driving the behemoth, but it did seem to be easier than the other day. She knew she would be in New Orleans soon, though, and the streets might not be so driver friendly to a vehicle as large as hers. Kate took a deep breath. As she saw she was getting closer to the city, she talked to herself, repeating the words, "I can do it." Soon her GPS started giving her directions to her new campsite for the next few days.

She had chosen a campground close to the city, knowing she could use taxis to go back and forth to the places she wanted to visit. She had a few friends who lived here, and she remembered several of the five-star hotels she had stayed in. Even though a part of her longed for that room service, she kept telling herself this trip was a good idea. One thing was for sure: this adventure of hers was completely different from anything she had ever experienced before.

She had already decided to do some very touristy attractions. The top of her list was the famous vampire tour. She had always heard about this but had never attended on her other visits to New Orleans. She also wanted to visit the French Quarter and downtown, two of her favorite places but had decided to refrain from Bourbon Street since she had already been there a few times before. Being completely by herself, just like her many trips before, Kate needed to be careful about where she went and mindful of the people she was around. She wasn't scared, but she wanted to be cautious. As for tonight, she would be fine because she was meeting Lena for dinner.

Kate and Lena met during Kate's first trip to New Orleans. She was the event director at a dinner Kate attended, and they had become fast friends, even if the friendship was mostly maintained through FaceTime chats, calls, and texts. In fact, Lena was the main reason Kate decided to make this first big stop in New Orleans. A familiar face before she continued west would feel good.

Kate made her way through the city streets, following every direction her GPS said. She went slowly at times, eliciting a honking car every now and then, but she didn't care. Finally she was at her new little camping spot. Only then did she realize how tightly she had gripped the steering wheel—to the point her knuckles were almost devoid of color. She also felt as if every muscle in her body had been on high alert. She felt tense and ready for action. She had been running an adrenaline as she was completely focused on arriving at her new campground safe and sound. Even though she was at her destination, she soon realized that she should have picked a campground away from the city, where this large moving box would have been much easier to drive.

The campground was much different from the first one she had stayed at. More trees, a larger camp store, nicer pool, and a bigger playground. Probably because it's closer to the city, she thought. Kate checked in and made her way to spot 77. As soon as she was parked, she hopped out to hook up everything outside, having gained a bit of confidence from her first night. As she reached the compartment where all the connections would be made to her little rolling home, she realized they were on the other side of the motor home!

"Hello?"

Kate turned around to see a smiling man. "Hi," Kate said tentatively.

"You must be new to the world of RVs," he said with a smile that never left his face.

"How could you tell?" Kate said with a bit of sarcasm in her voice.

"Well, you pulled into your spot instead of backing up. Backing up is the only way you'll have water and such, unless you use what's in your water tank and turn on the generator for electricity. If you do that, I don't think you'll make very many friends around here come nighttime."

Kate sighed and realized the gentleman was right. She only wished he hadn't been there to point out her mistake. "Silly me! Just wasn't paying attention. Let me get this thing parked correctly," Kate said as confidently as she could.

She did not want to let the man know she was a nervous wreck with the very idea of backing up a twenty-five-foot motor home into a space that looked even smaller than the one she had parked in before. Weren't all camping spaces supposed to be ones where she could just pull in and then out when needed? Apparently the answer was no because she was sitting in a space that was only one-way. She would write to the owners of this campground to make the suggestion that they remedy the situation, making it easier on their patrons for parking. She knew other RV owners would probably appreciate the convenience too.

"My name is Mike. If you want, I'll help you. Just watch me through your side mirrors, and we'll get you set up quick."

"Nice to meet you, Mike. I'm Kate." She stuck her hand out to shake his quickly. "I appreciate the help, but I think I can do it. Just wasn't paying attention when I pulled in."

Kate couldn't admit she needed help. Hadn't she done fine the first night? Plus, she had practiced this at home before her journey. It won't be hard, she thought.

"No problem, Miss Kate. Have yourself a nice day," Mike said, and she watched him walk down the little road.

Kate walked back and repositioned herself in the driver's seat, looking at both side mirrors. She took a deep breath. "You can do this," she said to generate some encouragement, but it wasn't helping.

Backing out of the space proved to be nerve-racking enough. How was she ever going to back up the motor home into the space correctly? A tiny feeling of defeat washed over her, but she took a deep breath and began the task before her.

As Kate looked from one side mirror to the other, she inched the large vehicle slowly backward. It seemed as if the hookups, picnic table, concrete patio, and anything else around her designated spot were just mere inches away from damaging the motor home. How many times now had she backed up and then pulled forward? She was beginning to lose count. Her neck was also tense and tight from looking constantly from one side mirror to the next. To the outsider, Kate probably looked as if she was watching a tennis match on her windshield.

"Whoa!" Kate suddenly heard very loudly.

She slammed on the brakes, hearing some of the items inside the motor home crash to the floor. When she looked in the mirror, she saw him. It was the cute guy from Biloxi. How in the world was he here?

"Pull forward again, and then turn your wheels slightly to the right," he said, and Kate was too shocked and mesmerized not to listen to the attractive man.

She was also grateful for the help. She realized now she should have accepted Mike's help earlier when he had offered.

"Now back up just a bit. Stop. Now straighten your wheels, and come straight back. I'll tell you when you are aligned with the hookups."

Kate did as she was told, never questioning the man, and before she knew it, she actually looked as if she was in line with the other campers on either side of her.

"Thank you so much," Kate said to the man as he walked up to the driver's door. "I think I was about to get there, but—" The sound of the man's laugh cut Kate off. This embarrassed her, but then her irritation grew by the second.

"No disrespect, but I think you would still be trying to get that thing in there for quite a while. Been watching you for at least twenty minutes already."

Kate's face was suddenly red. She felt the heat rise in her cheeks from frustration. He had been watching her? It seemed as if the little campground was mostly deserted of people for the day, and the thought that someone could have been watching made her feel slightly humiliated about her parking skills.

"Well, I'm glad I was able to give you some midday amusement. Rest assured, I would have eventually got the motor home parked and set up. I did great the other night."

"Is this your first camper?"

"Of course not!" Kate said defiantly, not wanting to tell the truth to this rugged, tantalizing stranger standing beside her now.

"What did you have before? A travel trailer? No, that wouldn't make sense because they can sometimes be a bit more challenging to back up."

Now he was making fun of her, which caused even more frustration to rise to the surface. As Kate looked at him, though, she was having a hard time developing the words she wanted to say.

Kate had watched this man from afar and then once close-up when she had the run-in with the door at the campground office, but now he was right here next to her. He was tall with a very muscular build that Kate noticed through his blue T-shirt. He had chocolate-brown hair and beautiful light-blue eyes. His angular chin showed he needed a shave, but the look suited him well. She couldn't take her eyes off him, but then she realized she was staring. But his good looks couldn't settle down the frustration she felt at his last comment.

"Now you are making fun of me? I thought people in campgrounds were supposed to be all nice and friendly. I guess you aren't in either group." There, she thought. Take that.

"I just helped you get that thing parked, and you are accusing me of being unfriendly? I was just kidding with you. People around here are supposed to be more relaxed. You don't seem to fit that description right now." The man stood there with a slight grin that was making it too hard for Kate to concentrate.

"Goodness, the compliments just keep flowing from your mouth like water from the river," she said quickly.

"I say we start over. Hi. I'm Brandon Anderson, and it's nice to meet you." He extended his hand out as to indicate that they start the conversation all over again.

Even though she was still a bit angry, Kate shook his hand. "OK. I'm Kate Palmer, and thank you for your assistance. And you are right. This is my first camper, but I don't own it. Just using it as I camp my way around the States."

"Wow! Someone let you borrow a motor home for a trip when you have never even traveled in one before? Sounds as if that person has a lot of confidence in you." Brandon now looked at her as if he was the nice neighbor instead of the heckler he appeared to be just moments ago.

"Long story. But thanks again. I need to finish putting things together and then head into the city."

"Then I better let you go. It was nice to meet you, Kate Palmer. Have fun and maybe I'll see you around."

Brandon walked off through the campsites, and she soon lost sight of him. What were the odds of him staying at her campground again? As she hooked up her camper to the necessities, including the smelly sewer hose, she couldn't help but think of the dashing man who had come to her rescue.

Four

"He sounds like a hottie to me," Lena said, and she took another bite of her shrimp creole.

"He was attractive but a smartass too. Making fun of me," Kate said. She took a sip of her drink and sat back in the chair, relaxing in the beautiful restaurant where the two friends had agreed to meet.

Kate had set up the camper pretty quickly after Brandon left and then hurriedly got dressed. Her taxi arrived just in time for her to get to the restaurant to meet Lena. They had spent most of the evening catching up, and then Kate gave her details of her first days out on the road.

"I'm really sorry to hear you and Thomas broke up. He was a nice guy," Lena said.

"It's really OK. When I started talking about the trip, it was as if both of us just realized we were good friends. Nothing more. So, I'm taking a break from dating while I travel the States. A little alone time for me. I actually didn't realize how much I rushed around all the time till yesterday morning at the campground. No agenda, meetings or timelines to meet. It felt odd but good at the same time. Never know—this trip might turn out to be a good thing but I miss my hotels."

"I think this is pretty cool what you are doing," Lena said. "Not many women like you would have taken on a challenge like this."

"What is that supposed to mean?" Kate said, her defensive side rising up for the second time that day.

"Kate, you know what I mean. You just admitted that you are a hotel and room service kinda girl. So am I! Camping doesn't appeal to me in the least. No desire whatsoever to pitch a tent or drive a…whatever you call that thing you are traveling in. Still hard for me to imagine you behind the wheel of some big old truck on the road," Lena said, and she smiled at her friend.

"I'm driving a motor home," Kate corrected her.

"Well, aren't you the smart one?" Lena glanced at Kate, who looked very serious about defending her position.

"To tell you the truth, it is still hard for me to believe. I will say, driving today was much easier than a couple of days ago, but at the campground I messed up parking and had to back that thing out of the spot. It took me at least thirty minutes! I was so embarrassed—especially since Brandon was watching me the whole time." Kate's cheeks flushed at the memory.

"So, his name is Brandon," her friend said slyly, and she looked at Kate with raised eyebrows.

"He is just the guy who helped me get that thing parked correctly so I could at least take a shower and use the toilet."

With that statement, Kate still cringed when she thought of the sewer hookup. She remembered the look on her father's face while the man at the dealership was giving her full instructions about what to do with the sewage system. She could tell from her father's facial expressions, especially his eyes as they crinkled at the edges, that he was laughing inside at the thought of his daughter performing such a feat. Kate also remembered sticking her tongue out at her dad while the man continued to give instructions.

"So, you are meeting some guys already?"

"Lena, please. Let's not go there."

"Why not! You met a good-looking guy today. Your words—not mine. I'm happy for you!" Lena said with a smile.

"I'm not looking for romance. This is a trip just for me," Kate said. "It will be nice to have some time alone. What about you? Who is the latest man in your life?" Kate asked. She was eager to take the focus off her and her love life.

"Nobody in particular right now. I've been so busy at work that when I do get some time off, I just want to go home, put on my pajamas, and not have to deal with anyone."

Kate could understand how Lena felt. Due to the type of job Lena had, she had to deal with the public—and a very picky group at that. Kate had heard Lena's stories of some of the clients that she had worked with and did not envy Lena's career choice at all. But her friend seemed to love what she did.

"This has been great, taking time to catch up with you in person!" Kate said with a smile. "But I think I should head back to the RV and put some time in on the computer. Need to put out a blog and do a bit of social media posting. I am taking the vampire tour tomorrow night. My readers are beyond excited that I decided to see the vampires of New Orleans. Wanna come with me?" Kate asked hopefully. "Those things kinda creep me out, but I'm trying to show I'm a hometown type of girl to my eager audience." With that last sentence, Kate forced a fake smile that had Lena laughing.

"I can't, but from what I've been told, you will love it. Everyone says those tours are great! Find someone at the campground to go with you. That would make a great read for your blog," Lena said as they walked out of the restaurant.

"That's not a bad idea. Everyone I've met so far seems pretty friendly."

"One more thing, Kate. Have fun with this trip. I know this is really new for you, but I think if you let yourself, you might just enjoy this whole adventure. I don't know of many people who get paid to travel all over the United States and see so many terrific places. Consider yourself blessed." With that, Lena gave her friend a big hug and took the next taxi that pulled up near the restaurant.

Kate stood there for a few moments and let Lena's words sink in.

She was right. I am so lucky I'm getting to do this, she thought. So, why don't I feel like it? Kate continued to ponder the words swirling in her head as she rode in the back of the taxi traveling back to the campground to her home on wheels.

Five

When the taxi pulled up to the front of the campground, Kate noticed everything except the general store seemed to be in complete darkness. There were just the occasional lights emanating from the various campers that gave a small bit of light to the campground. As she began to walk down the dark gravel road that led to her little camping spot, she began to realize how late it was. She was grateful most people seemed to be in bed because high heels and unpaved roads didn't mix. Several times her shoes caught on rocks, making her feet wobble. Kate was sure that if people were watching her, they would say she was hammered—too drunk to even walk. At that thought, she laughed and wanted to take the shoes off, but she was almost at her campsite and walking barefoot on gravel would be too painful. Though it felt good to dress up in the clothes she was most used to, a pair of sneakers would have been much more comfortable and probably safer for her ankles. Once again, she broke out in laughter just imagining the sight of her graceful walk to the RV.

As morning dawned, the local campground food smells made their way into the motor home again. This time, they seemed stronger than before. Kate had only imagined microwave dinners, fast food stops, and hopefully some nice restaurants along the way—not much home cooking for months. The aroma from outside was so enticing, though. According to her phone, it was 6:30 a.m. She lay in bed, deciding to just take her time and enjoy the morning. There was no rushing around because she wasn't on a strict timeline. This world was all so new to her, and that tiny part of her began to think again that this might not have been such an awful idea after all. She refused to give in to the thought just yet.

Today, she was going to do some work during the morning, followed by treating herself to some tourist time at the French Quarter, a quick dinner, and then the infamous vampire tour. Her only regret right now was she didn't have someone to share it with. She would be with a group, though, like she had been in the larger cities she had traveled to. There had to be someone she could talk to. She especially wanted a companion on this tour since this whole vampire thing made her a bit anxious. The tour information reminded her of the Ghost Tours they had back home in Charleston, which she had only experienced once because of the creepy feeling she had after going on one with a friend. But her readers were so excited, though, and had been waiting on a full report of her day once she told them of her plans.

As she took a break from writing and answering e-mails, she walked to the camp store to stretch her legs and actually see what they had to offer. At least this time walking down the road she was steadier on her feet. She was wearing her slip-on shoes paired with jeans and a T-shirt. Earlier, as Kate laid out her clothes for the day, she couldn't remember the last time she had dressed so casual during travel, but it actually felt good. She would change before going into the city, but dressed as she was, it reminded her of her childhood.

"So, you were able to get all hooked up. Is everything working fine?" she heard from behind her.

Kate turned to see Brandon at his campsite. His van was pulled so far back that she hadn't noticed it the day before.

"I did. And I do want to thank you again for your help yesterday. Even though I think I would have finally gotten it parked correctly."

Brandon did that same laugh again. "I'm glad to see you have confidence in yourself. That is always a good thing when you are learning something new. It's okay to be a newbie to the camping world. You will get the hang of it," Brandon said, and he fell in step beside her.

"Why does everyone keep saying that? I feel as if I'm on display or something." Kate was feeling embarrassed once more.

"Hey, at some point, all of us were in your shoes. Well, maybe not your high heels."

Kate felt the color drain from her face. He had to have seen her wobbly, awkward walk to her camper last night. "What are you talking about?" she said, feigning innocence.

"Last night I thought you were pretty drunk till I saw you all dressed up with those heels on. It's a wonder you didn't break your ankle the way you were walking last night. You must have hit every piece of gravel on the road." Brandon chuckled once more, and Kate blushed as they continued their walk toward the store.

"No, I wasn't drunk. But why were you spying on me?"

"I wasn't spying on you. I was sitting outside and enjoying the evening. You just happened to walk by. That is to say, wobble by."

"Do you enjoy making fun of people?" Kate said. She wanted to be irritated at his remark but found it hard to keep the feeling each time she glanced in his direction.

"You're right. I'll stop. But watching you walk to your camper last night was the highlight of my evening."

"Well, tonight I'm wearing more appropriate clothing. Jeans, shirt, jacket, and flats for sure," Kate said. This time she laughed herself. She knew Brandon's assessment of her walk home the night before was right.

"So, what grand plans do you have for this evening?" he asked, and he held the door to the store open for her to enter.

"Sight-seeing this afternoon and a vampire tour this evening."

"A vampire tour? Is this your first time in New Orleans?"

"No, I have been here plenty of times, but I've never been on a vampire tour. My readers can't wait for me to let them know what I think about it," Kate said.

"Your readers?"

"I have a travel blog. I'm keeping them up to date on the adventures of my camping trip."

"How many readers?" Brandon asked, and he grabbed a Push-Up ice cream out of the freezer. He took the paper off to start eating it before it was even paid for.

Kate grabbed one too and followed his lead. "Long story short, I have a travel blog, and one of my readers challenged me to see America instead of doing another trip to another city out of the country. Said I needed to experience small-town USA. Before I knew it, an RV dealership offered to lend me the use of a motor home for the trip, I had sponsors on my blog, and my readership went through the roof. Everyone was so excited. Except me."

"So, you are one of those girls who likes to fly, stay in expensive hotels, and ride in taxis—or, I bet, better yet—limos."

"Is that so bad?" Kate asked. She felt exasperated once again.

"I guess not, but I mean, a free RV to use for travel? You don't seem that excited. That's for sure. You are basically getting paid to travel. There are a lot of people who would love to be in your shoes. Just not the high heels," Brandon said with a smile.

"Ha-ha." Kate sighed and smiled back. "The idea of the trip is growing on me just a little. And quit making fun of my shoes." Kate paused and had a thought. "Do you have any plans tonight? How would you like to go on the vampire tour with me? My treat. I really don't want to go by myself." Once the words were out of her mouth, she couldn't believe she had asked a total stranger to practically go on a date. She quickly added, "Just as friends."

"We are friends now?" Brandon asked, turning his head to the side to look at her.

"Well, you did help me park my camper. Then you secretly watched me walk home last night, and now we are having an ice cream together. You are my first official campground friend. No, make that the third. I met Jean and Henry in Biloxi."

"I'm not much into vampires, but it sounds like it could be fun. I have some work to do, so I'll meet you in the city tonight."

"Sounds like a date!" Kate said, once again putting her foot in her mouth.

"A date?" Brandon said with raised eyebrows.

"You know what I mean," Kate said, and she walked out of the little store and back toward her camper.

She felt lighter and a bit excited. The sexy mystery man she had spotted on her first day of camping was no longer a mystery and was now going on a tour with her in the city. She shouldn't be feeling this excited since she had just recently declared this trip a "no man" zone, but she couldn't help it. He was gorgeous and sexy, and even though he liked to tease her, she enjoyed being around him. And the way he made her feel—a different sort of happiness she couldn't explain just yet.

A ringing phone in her pocket suddenly caught her attention. As she looked at the screen, she began to wonder why Thomas would be calling her.

Six

"Hi," Thomas said before Kate could answer her phone.

"Hello yourself. How are you doing?"

"Fine. Just checking up on you. According to your blog, I see you're in New Orleans. Having fun?"

"So far I'm doing OK. It is definitely a learning experience," Kate said. "How are you?"

"Same old thing here. You are the one having the adventure. Meet any guys out there?" Thomas asked.

"Why would you ask me that?"

"Just kidding with you. You know that. I know we are just friends, but I do miss you, Kate. We did have fun when we were dating. At least, I thought we did."

"Of course we did. Remember that time we went skiing? I thought for sure I would come home with a broken leg. Thank goodness snow is soft, or my tailbone would have been broken for sure." Kate laughed. They might not be dating, but Thomas was a good friend, and their time together was fun for her too.

"Ah, yes. Skiing. You lied to me and told me you had been before."

"I thought we would get there, and I could make some excuse to just sit in the lodge. But, oh no. You were persistent, and I was caught red-handed." Kate sighed, and Thomas was silent. "Listen, I gotta go. Getting ready to go into town. I'm taking a vampire tour tonight, if you can believe that. I'm going in early to do some sightseeing on foot, which is different for me too. Kinda looking forward to it."

"I miss you, Kate," Thomas said. His voice sounded a bit melancholy.

"Miss you too, Thomas. Tell everyone I said hi." With that, Kate hung up the phone, and her excitement turned to her upcoming evening with Brandon.

* * *

*K*ate loved the French Quarter of New Orleans. She had been there several times, but this time was totally different. She was more relaxed because she didn't have an agenda to adhere to like most of the trips she took before. She was actually able to stroll through Jackson Square, taking time to watch the many street performers and get lost in their talents. The artists lining the walkway were many, and Kate was mesmerized watching all of them create their latest masterpieces. Why had she not seen this before? She had been here many times, but it seemed as if she was seeing everything around her for the very first time.

She purchased a few of New Orleans's famous beignets for a snack and then went to sit at the park situated along the Mississippi River. She watched the boats float by and observed people, being able to tell the difference between who was a tourist and who was a local. This was one of her favorite pastimes when she had a chance to just sit and relax.

Kate could feel she was finally starting to unwind a little. Well, at least when she wasn't behind the wheel of Monster. Things felt peaceful—except for the little tug in the back of her mind about Thomas. He sounded different this morning during their conversation, and she couldn't quite explain the feeling it had given her inside. She missed him as a friend, but her intuition and the sound of Thomas's voice gave her the impression he might not be feeling the same way. Kate, you are just making something of out nothing, she admonished herself. They had both come to the same conclusion before she left, and she knew then she was probably just a bit homesick. Then she remembered the man she was about to spend the evening with, and those unsettled feelings began to fade away quickly.

Nothing romantic, right? She kept telling herself it was only a friend date, and they were traveling two separate paths. It was just a coincidence they were staying in the same campground for the second time. It was, however, a nice coincidence. At that thought, she quickly chided herself. Remember your "no dating—no men" rule? she thought. But as she ruminated over in her mind about the restriction she had put on herself, maybe she didn't have to have such a steadfast rule. Maybe she could just try to let things flow, not force anything, one way or another. Kate had always had this routine, these guidelines, that she stuck to like glue. Maybe this trip would change all that for her.

Kate continued to sit on the bench, lost in thought. Then she realized the sun was starting to set, and with a quick look at her phone, she knew she needed to grab something to eat before meeting Brandon for the tour. As a matter of fact, she only had forty-five minutes before starting to walk the streets where vampires once roamed, so she was told. As it became darker, she made her way toward St. Louis Cathedral. After spending such a leisurely afternoon along the square, she got a small drink and some french fries to munch on. She walked, enjoying the beautiful evening and feeling the most relaxed she had since leaving on this trip. She could see people gathering for the tour as she walked toward the church. Maybe Brandon wouldn't show up. That would be fine with her. Well, honestly, no. It wouldn't, Kate admitted. She was really looking forward to seeing him and maybe even getting to know him better. This was all research, though, she told herself. Nothing more. She was trying to sound convincing to herself but to little avail.

"Is this the biting line?" Kate heard right in her ear.

The sound of the male voice startled her so badly that she flung her drink straight up into the air. Its contents came splashing down on her shoulder and she looked over to see Brandon's shirt covered in her drink. She was horrified that she was so on edge that a simple remark had caused this predicament. Now she and her new friend were trying to dry off with the napkins she still had in her hand from the french fry vendor.

"I'm so sorry! I didn't mean to scare you like that. Are you always this jumpy?" Brandon said, as he tried to dry his shirt with the flimsy paper napkins Kate had given him but they were disintegrating as fast as he could use them. He then took one of the napkins and wiped some of the liquid off her shoulder, taking special notice of her creamy, soft skin.

"No, you just scared me. Anyway, it's getting dark, and for goodness' sake, this is a vampire tour!" Kate said, trying to pull herself together quickly, but she had noticed how Brandon had helped her, and the touch of his hand on her arm did not go unnoticed.

"Maybe you shouldn't do this. You know they have tales of real vampires here," he said in a husky voice. He was trying to sound scary, but it had the opposite effect on Kate. It made him sound sexy and very appealing.

"I'm sure everything is fictional. Besides, I have to write about this tomorrow. I have readers who have been tweeting all day about my tour tonight."

"That's right—your fans. Whatever would happen if you didn't live up to their expectations?"

"Now you are mocking me?" Kate said defensively, but she could tell by the look on Brandon's face that he was kidding with her once again.

"I would never do that. But I think we need to go. They're getting ready to leave without us," he said, and he suddenly grabbed her hand and pulled her quickly toward the group. An electric current seemed to run between both of them, and when they looked at each other, they knew they were feeling the same way. "We have to hurry!"

They showed their paid receipts to the tour guide and began the walk, keeping toward the back of the large group. Each place they stopped, the tour guide told them of a supposed real or fictional vampire who had once walked the famous streets of New Orleans. It was beginning to make Kate feel just a bit uneasy inside. Especially with the surrounding darkness, the stories seemed more ominous and real. She was secretly glad Brandon was with her. He made her feel safe, even though she was surrounded by at least twenty-five other people. The rest of their tour group were strangers, but at least she knew one person, and he was right by her side. Brandon was so close that she could feel the heat coming off his body.

Kate wanted to ask him more questions about his life, why he was camping, where he was heading, and what seemed a million more things, but each time she started to talk, the tour guide had more eerie tales to share with the group. Still, having him there with her made the whole tour so much more enjoyable than she had expected.

"I can now say I know so much more about vampires. Plus, my shirt is nice and dry. So, where do we go now?" Brandon asked as the tour came to an end and people went their separate ways.

"I'm heading back to the campground and hoping that I don't have nightmares," Kate said remembering many of the creepy tales but so glad she had taken the tour. "Want to catch a taxi with me?"

"Sounds good, but why don't we take the city bus? It's cheaper and will drop us off about a half mile from the campground. I probably should get back as well since I'm leaving early in the morning."

Kate had two thoughts at once: one, he was already leaving, and she didn't want him to, and two, there was no way she was riding on a city bus.

"A bus?" Kate said. She always used taxis, except for a few exceptions on a subway, and that had only been for the experience.

Buses just seemed so nasty or dirty. Those were the only words coming to Kate's mind.

"You don't ride buses? You do travel to all these big cities, right?" Brandon looked at her in surprise.

"Of course I ride buses." OK. Now she had lied. Wait, she thought. No. I rode a bus in London a few years ago and one in Paris.

"Let's head to the bus stop. It should be here shortly," Brandon said, and they walked along the city street.

Reluctantly, Kate followed because she didn't want to appear as if a bus ride was beneath her. Mostly, though, she wanted to be with Brandon.

"So, where is your next stop on your camping trip?" Kate asked as soon as she sat down on the bus seat right beside Brandon. She did not want to sit beside the other people, and she immediately noticed the bus wasn't as dirty as she had imagined.

"Galveston, Texas. Going to spend a few days on the beach. Ever been there?"

"No. I hear it's beautiful, though."

"What about you? Where is your next stop?"

"I'm leaving tomorrow too but not so early. Heading to San Antonio. I've been before but only for conferences. Never did any sight-seeing, and I was told I have to go to the River Walk and the Alamo."

"From your readers again?" Brandon said with a smile as the bus lurched forward to the next stop.

"Yep. Sometimes I feel as if they are directing this trip instead of me," Kate said with a laugh.

"Maybe that's a good thing."

"What do you mean?"

"From what you have shared with me, you've been to the bigger cities but never to some of these smaller towns. Even in the big cities, you have never experienced some of the simpler things. They are just giving you suggestions. Would you have ever gone on a vampire tour?" he asked.

"Honestly, no." Brandon was right. She was doing things so completely out of her comfort zone and though Kate wouldn't say it out loud, she had to admit she was having a little bit of fun.

"That's a long drive from here to San Antonio. About eight hours. Are you doing it all in one day?"

"Not this time. My first day on this crazy trip, I had the grand idea I could go from Spartanburg, South Carolina, to Biloxi, Mississippi, no problem at all. I learned my lesson quick on that one. Google Maps said eight hours, but it was an eleven-hour ride for me. I think I'm going to stop in Beaumont, Texas. Another reader said it was nice there." Kate stopped, hoping Brandon might have some input on her selection of cities. Maybe he'd even say he had changed his mind and would go to San Antonio.

"I should make Galveston by late afternoon."

"How long have you been on the road?" Kate really wanted to know more about this man and the trip he was on. Him sitting so close to her on the bus seat sent shivers through her. She tried to ignore them but couldn't any longer. She began to notice all the little features of his face, especially the beautiful blue eyes, every time he looked at her. She noticed the way his arm and leg pressed gently against her. He felt taut and toned.

"For a while." This was the only answer Kate received as they continued on their journey to the campground.

"Oh." I guess the subject isn't up for discussion, Kate thought. "So, what do you do?" she asked, trying to change the subject.

"Just travel."

"You don't work?"

"A little here and there."

Kate couldn't believe how much Brandon had clammed up with what she considered simple personal questions. She probably seemed like an open book to him. She had answered all his questions so neatly. Why couldn't he share some details like she had?"Interesting." It was all she could think of saying as the bus stopped at their destination.

"I had a really good time tonight," Brandon said, breaking the awkward silence that had developed as they walked toward the campground. "I know to make sure not to sneak up on you, even if only to say hi," he said gesturing to his shirt, "and that I should be careful of the vampires that could still be lurking around New Orleans. Though I have been here several times without incident."

Kate couldn't help but blush at his statement. "I really am sorry about the drink. Thank goodness it wasn't one of those red slushies. People would have thought you were part of the tour," she laughed and looked at Brandon to see him flash his dashing smile at her. "But I had a nice time too. Thanks for going with me. Now to navigate the confines of my miniscule shower," Kate said with a sigh. Suddenly she was thinking of the tiny bathroom and comparing it to the larger rooms of the hotels she was so fond of.

"Use the bathhouse. Plenty of room there," Brandon said.

"No way! It's nasty. Using a shower with hundreds of other people. Full of germs. I've heard you can get terrible foot fungus in those showers. I was warned to wear flip-flops if I had to use them. Someone else told me they are usually filled with bugs of all sorts. The worst, though, is that people get kidnapped—especially if you are there by yourself. I think I'll stick with my telephone booth shower, thank you very much." When she finally calmed down, she saw Brandon was laughing way too hard at her expense. "What is so funny?" she said, stopping on the gravel road leading to their campsites. She placed both hands on her hips defiantly as though defending her position.

"You believe all that stuff?"

"Someone must have experienced these things. I don't think they invented those stories out of thin air."

"Kate, I know you haven't been on the road that long, but have you been in a bathhouse yet?"

"No, and I don't plan to. I have promised myself the luxury of a hotel every now and then on this trip, and that's when I'll get my leisurely bath and shower time."

"OK, but really, they aren't that bad. I use them at every campground. I don't have the *luxury* of having my own telephone booth shower." Brandon said the words with a bit of sarcasm that didn't escape Kate.

Now she was a bit perturbed. "Are you making fun of me again?"

"I'm sorry. I'm just trying to picture how you are going to make it the rest of your trip. You have a lot to learn about camping,

Kate. Actually, I think you are "glamping". Once you get the hang of it, though, I think you're going to fall in love with it."

"What do you mean by glamping?" Kate was now irritated with the man walking with her.

"I don't know the exact definition but basically you go camping to enjoy the great outdoors but your take all your luxuries with you. That's you."

Kate suddenly realized they were standing in front of her motor home. "It doesn't feel like I'm 'glamping' as you called it because I don't have all my *luxuries* with me. As for falling in love with camping? Not sure I can agree with you on that, but I do know I can do it for six months." Kate looked down at the ground, starting to calm down a bit and looked up, back into Brandon's eyes. They were now illuminated by the full moon above and all the irritation she had just had with him seemed to slowly disappear. "Thanks for sharing the evening with me. Once again, I had a great time, and I hope you enjoy Galveston."

"You have fun on your glamping odyssey and I mean that with all sincerity. You're going to love small-town America. It's simpler than your fancy resorts but more fulfilling." He reached out his hand for a friendly shake.

When Kate took it, she felt that same pulse of electricity as it traveled up her arm and spread to the rest of her body. Then she watched him walk away toward his tent. She suddenly had the urge to follow him to Galveston. Ugh! she thought. I just met the man! What am I thinking! She knew exactly what she was thinking. She didn't want him to go. Kate had thoroughly enjoyed his company tonight. She had been so alone on this trip, and tonight it had been nice to have someone to talk to. It was an added bonus that he just happened to be a very good-looking man.

As she entered the camper, sat down, and looked around her, that feeling of homesickness enveloped her again. Was she really going to be able to complete this trip like she had boasted to Brandon? Did she even want to? It seemed like her feelings about this adventure bounced from good to bad to good again, depending on her circumstances.

Kate continued to toss the thoughts of Brandon and her hometown back and forth in her mind as she took her shower. As she reached for her bottle of liquid soap, she accidently hit it, sending the small container directly into the toilet. "You have got to be kidding! Could they make this space any smaller?" she said aloud in frustration, feeling a little defeated.

Now she would have to buy more soap. Great! If only she had lowered the lid, it wouldn't be in the toilet bowl now. Maybe next time she would brave the bathhouse. She'd just make sure to have a can of Raid in one hand and Mace in the other.

Seven

As Kate walked to the campground store the next morning, the first thing she noticed was the empty spot where Brandon's van and tent once were. She could feel the tiny disappointment inside knowing he was already gone and they wouldn't see each other again. Maybe this is how it works when you camp, she thought. Some people you meet only a brief time. A part of her hoped that maybe, especially after her dinner with Jean and Henry the other night, she would make new friends. Before she had left Jean the other day, they had exchanged e-mail addresses and became friends on Facebook. Kate smiled at the memory, but the smile faded to just a thin line knowing Brandon wouldn't be one of those friends. If she had already met this many people so far on her trip, though, she was sure there would be more along the way.

Kate checked the map on her iPad before pulling out of the campground. She contemplated trying to make it to San Antonio but once again the thought of an eight-hour trip wasn't the least bit appealing to Kate. As she had told Brandon last night, she would stick to her destination of Beaumont, Texas. According to the map before her, it seemed maybe halfway. She made sure her GPS app was guiding her, and she checked that everything she needed was around her driving area but nestled safely: a drink in the cup holder, her phone in its designated place, and a few snacks. For some odd reason, as Kate pulled out onto the busy street to head west, she felt as though this was the true beginning of her camping trip. It had already been days since she picked up the borrowed camper from the dealership, but she had looked at the map once more, before making her right hand turn, and she was truly heading west now. She would be going through towns and places she had only flown over before. Kate felt a rush of excitement. This was totally different from that first day when she climbed in the driver's seat to start this journey and waved good-bye to her dad and Thomas. That day, Kate recalled, she just wanted this stupid trip to be over with. She had wondered if she should have just ignored or made jokes about Bubba's blog comment. Driving now on Interstate 10 toward Texas, Kate also remembered that part of her hadn't wanted to back down from the challenge.

Kate had learned one lesson already. As she pulled out of the camping spot this morning, several people guided her. She gladly accepted the help. The fiasco a few days ago taught her that she didn't have to know it all. It was OK to be new to this outdoor world. The people who camped around her were more than friendly. They all seemed to help each other, shared hellos as they walked by, or had conversations about everything from the latest place to stay to the best tourist attraction in the city. It was truly a different world—like nothing she had experienced before.

As Kate traveled down the interstate, she was crossing over beautiful bayous. The scenery seemed to change so much and was not at all as expected. She did her best to stay in the right lane, driving the speed limit only and made sure to let the large semi trucks pass. They still gave her that "crap, they are too close" feeling and caused the motor home to sway. The longer she was on the road, though, the more she became used to the feeling. She knew what to expect when she saw one of the large trucks in her side mirror getting ready to pass her.

The "Texas Welcome Center" sign was soon in her sights. Yes, thank goodness, Kate thought. She could have stopped before now, but each time she passed an exit, she kept thinking she could make it just a little farther before stopping to use the bathroom. Heck, she could just pull off the exit, find a parking lot, and use the one in the camper!

As she crossed the state line, she couldn't believe she was alone in Texas in a motor home. When she saw the huge sliver star that greeted all visitors to the Lone Star State, though, she knew she was there, and a feeling of happiness flooded through her.

Kate followed the signs for RV parking which happened to be the same area for those trucks she dreaded on the highway. She had to park right alongside the massive semi trucks but at least the parking spaces were long and very wide. As soon as she used the camper bathroom, she stood outside for a moment and just stretched. The sun felt warm and inviting. And the breeze in the air felt good on her skin. The center was beautiful, and she looked around at the unique wetlands area. It seemed the building was built over a bayou with walkways that allowed people to stroll through the area. As she walked toward the building, she immediately saw it: the VW van she had looked for this morning. No way! Was Brandon here? They seemed to be running into each other a lot, but then again, they were both heading to Texas. She thought he would be in Galveston by now, having left so much earlier than she had.

As Kate walked into the Welcome Center, she picked up a few Texas brochures from the rack near the entrance. She especially focused on anything pertaining to her journey west along Interstate 10. Really, though, she was looking from side to side as inconspicuously as she could, searching for any sign of Brandon but she didn't see him anywhere. Maybe he was in the bathroom or outside on the walkways over the swamp. Maybe it wasn't his van, she thought suddenly. It sure looked like it, though. Kate had secretly hoped it was because the moment it came into view, a spark of joy made her whole body tingle with excitement. She looked and looked, and he was nowhere to be found. Wishful thinking, Kate thought to herself, and she headed outside to walk the wooden trails high above the marsh area below.

The wooden walkways were about ten feet above the ground. They gave visitors a great way to observe the wildlife below, which included a very large snake that had Kate backing up as soon as it came into her view. Her fear of the snake completely wiped out the rest of the beauty around her.

"I thought that was you," Kate heard as she bumped into someone and nearly fell backward. She was caught in a pair of very strong, muscular arms. They wrapped around her gently. "And I was right."

She looked up to see Brandon's electric blue eyes once again. "Goodness, you scared me. The snake below already had me heading back into the building," Kate said in a rush.

"He's too far away to bother you. Anyway, it looks as if he has already eaten for the day."

Kate dared to look back at the snake once more and saw what Brandon was referring to: a large mass in the snake's thin body.

"Well, I don't care. Snakes are snakes, and this girl stays away from them like the plague! They give me the creeps! Actually all creepy, crawly things do."

"And you're heading west? Camping? In rattlesnake country? You know, they even have rattlesnake roundups here. Kinda like festivals," Brandon said cheerfully as they walked back toward the building.

"You have got to be kidding!" Kate said incredulously.

"That's what they are called—rattlesnake roundups. Very popular," he said for emphasis.

"My readers won't be reading about that in my blog. That's for sure. And don't start with me again about the camping thing. I've done quite well so far this morning." Kate looked over to see Brandon with a slight grin, and this caused her to smile.

"Don't you really mean 'glamping'?"

Kate rolled her eyes. "For your information, I did some research on 'glamping'. I guess you could say that I do fall into the category just a bit but to me it's all just camping."

"You are so much fun to tease. I bet you even have wine glasses in your camper," Brandon said as he grinned at her.

"As a matter of fact I do."

"Then it's official: you are a glamper."

"Well, whatever you want to say, I'm camping and like I said earlier, so far so good."

"Oh, you will do fine," he said and looked at her sweetly as he opened the door to the building once again.

"I thought you would be way ahead of me. Aren't you heading south?"

"Yep. Just made a few stops on the way here and thought I'd take a quick break before heading to the beach."

Kate couldn't help but stare at the attractive man as they stood inside the welcome center even though she did her best to act as uninterested as possible.

"Camping on the beach? That sounds fun," she said, thinking that it really did sound like a great idea. Maybe she could do that on the coast in California. Then she suddenly had the image of her RV on the beach with Brandon by her side. Not happening, Kate, she told herself.

"The beaches in Galveston are great but there are more places along the Texas Gulf Coast that are nice too. Might start in Galveston and just work my way south toward Mexico. No plans just yet."

"It's great you have the ability to just go wherever you want. You never did tell me what you did for a living," Kate asked anxiously, wondering if she would get a short, vague answer like before when she asked him questions

"I'm a consultant. Of sorts. It allows me to travel as long as I have my laptop with me," Brandon said. He opened the front entrance door for her and gave her a wink.

"So, you live by a laptop too. Ten years ago, I never would have imagined I would make my living writing on the Internet, sharing information. I didn't even know what a blog was!" Kate said. She hoped that if she shared more facts about herself, he might do the same.

"I sure love working this way because it does give us some freedom that most people don't have. Look at you. Free motor home and sponsors to pay your expenses to travel and see this country. Lots of people would give just about anything to be in your shoes. Well, almost all of your shoes," Brandon said. He laughed and made her remember the wobbly walk along the campground road her first night in New Orleans.

"I love those shoes, but I'll just have to save them for Las Vegas," Kate said with a smile.

"Going to Vegas? Love it there!"

"I do too. Just never stayed there in a camper before. That's why it's going to be one of my splurge cities."

"Splurge cities?"

"I promised myself I would stay in a few hotels along the way. In Vegas, I'm going to stay at my favorite: the Bellagio. That is usually where I stay when I'm in town."

"And what will your readers think?"

"I haven't decided what to tell them just yet."

"What about just telling them the truth? You are taking a camping break. Nothing wrong with that," Brandon said as he stopped on the sidewalk.

Kate suddenly felt self-conscious. Did she sound like a stuck-up snob? She hoped not. That certainly wasn't her intention. She really just wanted to keep talking to him. She didn't want him to go. She felt drawn to this man and truly enjoyed his company, even if they had only met a few days ago. In the back of her mind, though, she knew this was just a passing thing. They were moving in different directions and probably wouldn't see each other again.

"So, you are heading to San Antonio?" Brandon said. "That's not a small town. I thought your readers wanted you to do something different."

It seemed Brandon had been listening to her. "From what I can gather, they just wanted me to do something different than my typical travel: high-dollar hotels, first-class flying, and world travel."

"Well, you can definitely say you've changed your travel style. And the longer you're out here, the more you'll find you will like being on the road. So much to see, do, and experience," Brandon said as though he was recalling a memory or two. "By the way, there is a real nice campground right outside San Antonio. It's close to the city and just off the interstate. Easy to take a taxi, so you won't have to take a city bus," he said as he laughed while Kate just smirked at him.

"Thanks for the info," she said. There suddenly seemed to be an awkward silence, like neither one of them wanted to say goodbye but their vehicles were in opposite directions.

"Glad I ran into you again, Kate. Enjoy America." Brandon gave her another wink and turned to walk away.

Kate couldn't help but watch him as he walked. She noticed more things about him: his gait, his tan, and the arms that had caught her only a short while ago. Then he looked back to see her staring, and Kate felt the heat rush to her face.

She slowly turned around and shut her eyes as she shook her head. She wondered what had gotten into her. Flirting with someone who was practically a stranger? Wishing so much he was going her way instead of his? As she climbed back into the driver's seat, though, she smiled. All she could think about was the ruggedly handsome face of the stranger she had first seen in Biloxi and how, for some reason, their paths kept crossing.

Eight

As Brandon pulled out of the Welcome Center, he looked back in the rearview mirror to see if he could get one more glance of Kate. Damn, she was making this hard. She was nothing like what he had expected when he got the phone call from his father, the one he almost ignored. But for some reason, he answered and now found himself in this jam. Should he follow her, like he agreed to do, or just call back and tell his father the deal was off? That was what he had decided this morning but seeing her again at the center was making him doubt his decision.

Traveling down the road that led him to the coast of Texas, Brandon couldn't get Kate out of his mind. She was different than any girl he had met before. Her charming personality shown through her "trying to be confident" exterior. But her golden blonde hair and the hazel green eyes had him entranced. Plus he had seen her in a beautiful cocktail dress one night and tee shirt with shorts the next day—both outfits hugging her body in all the right places. Her skin hinted at a bit of a tan and he remembered the softness of it from the other night after he helped her clean up the drink she had spilled on the both of them.

Brandon checked into the campground by the beach and proceeded to set up his tent as usual. He had to admit he was attracted to Kate but there was no way he could do what his father had asked. So tomorrow morning, he would call to let him know that the deal was off and he was going back to his original plan of heading to Florida for a while. He needed to get as far away as he could from Arizona and what was being asked of him took him closer to home instead. He needed time to think and regroup. That had been the whole purpose of leaving home after what had happened. But now a stunning woman had been thrown into the mix of emotions he was feeling and if he was honest, Brandon was thinking more about her than anything else. Maybe some sleep would help him clear his head then he would head back east in the morning.

* * *

Kate drove into the campground in Beaumont, Texas, knowing ahead of time they had those pull-through campsites. After the frustration of parking Monster at the last campground in New Orleans, she determined this was a necessary thing for the rest of her trip. She arrived in the late afternoon along with other campers stopping for the night. As she waited in line for her turn at the check-in counter, she felt a small tap on her shoulder. "Are you Kate Palmer?"

She turned to see a very striking woman. She was about the same height as Kate but older. She was standing beside Kate and had a tiny white dog cradled in her arms. Before Kate could utter a word, the woman began speaking excitedly. "It is you! I just knew it! I recognized you from the picture on your blog. I've been reading about your camping adventure, and I wondered if we might meet you since we were traveling the same highway. Told my husband all about you. My mom thinks it's fantastic what you're doing. Oh, by the way, my name is Laurie Madden." The woman held out her hand to Kate, which Kate proceeded to shake.

This feels so weird, Kate thought. People recognizing me from a blog?

"My husband is checking us in now. We are heading to San Antonio, but there was no way he was going to drive through Houston during rush hour. Except to me it seems pretty busy all day in that area. So, how are you enjoying the RV lifestyle so far?"

Kate suddenly wasn't thinking about the woman standing with her but the cars, trucks, and more she would face in the much bigger cities she and her dad had planned for her to travel through. She had visited Houston before, and it was pretty intense with its myriad of highways. However, it had never bothered her because she had always been in a taxi or limo. She remembered only how much she loved it there. Kate could feel her breathing speed up at the thought of driving Monster through the huge city.

"I'm sorry. I didn't catch what you said," Kate said quickly when she saw Laurie staring at her.

"The RV—how are you adjusting? To tell you the truth, I'm a hotel girl, but my husband and mother love camping. So, we compromised and bought a motor home with all the bells and whistles. I get my bit of luxury, and they get to do all the outdoorsy stuff."

As the woman talked, Kate stood there and just listened. Even though Kate hadn't been able to say much, she felt like she had found a kindred spirit in Laurie. Both of them preferring hotels, Kate wondered how Laurie adjusted to this camping lifestyle. She suddenly thought she just might get along with this woman. Kate had been pretty adamant about her travels before and had expressed her displeasure about this whole camping trip because it would be so out of the norm for her. As Kate thought about it now, taking care of the motor home was becoming a bit routine. A routine, she admitted silently, was almost nice, but she was not fully ready to voice that out loud to anyone.

"I think I'm doing well so far. Still have much to learn, but it's giving me plenty of information for my blog posts."

Just then, a nice-looking older gentleman came to stand beside Laurie.

"Darling, this is Kate—the girl online who is writing about her camping experience. Remember? I told you about her. She's like me. Give me a resort and valet parking any day." Laurie reached up and gave the man a quick kiss on the cheek.

The man smiled warmly at his wife and then at Kate, who found herself once again shaking hands with another stranger.

"Hi, I'm Richard, and it's nice to meet you. My wife here has been going on and on about you. If you need anything, just let us know. We are in site number thirty-eight. Having steaks tonight on the grill, and you are officially invited. Would love to talk about your adventure so far and where you are heading. Hell, maybe we'll even do a story on you!"

"We own several magazines and newspapers. Think what you're doing is fascinating," Laurie said.

Kate stood there a bit shocked. Magazines? Newspapers?

"Please say you'll come to dinner," Laurie said with almost a pout on her face.

At the rate she had been asked to campground dinners, Kate wouldn't have to do much cooking in her motor home! "Thanks. That sounds wonderful," Kate said with a bit of hesitation but a smile on her face. "Is there anything I can bring?"

"Just yourself!" Laurie said.

Kate had planned on a nice evening in bed reading or watching television, if she could just figure out how to get it to work. The gentleman at the dealership had made things look so easy as far as operating everything in the camper but so far on her journey, she had been unsuccessful in her attempts to use the TV. But this was all she had planned after a quick dinner from the microwave.

"Let's say six o'clock. Does that sound OK, Kate?" Laurie said in a sweet, Southern accent. She wrapped one arm around her husband, and the other still contained the cute little dog.

"See you then," Kate said, and she watched the couple walk away. She still couldn't fathom the fact that people recognized her from a blog on the Internet. *At least I'm getting some free dinners out of this,* she thought and laughed to herself as the line moved. She was next to check in to her new little camp spot for the night.

* * *

*T*hank goodness, Kate thought as she climbed the steps into the motor home. As promised, she had been able to pull straight into her camp space—no backing up required. Also, it was bigger than the other two campgrounds she had visited so far. She hooked up the motor home once more. This time was a little easier, and she was beginning to see the sewer hose was not her enemy. However, she still donned the disposable gloves. Maybe when she got to San Antonio for a few days, she would attempt to put that thing out that was attached to the side of the motor home. It was called the awning if her memory served her correctly. It would cover the entrance door to the motor home, giving her shade along the side from the hot Texas sun. In truth, though, she had already forgotten how it worked. The way everyone had been friendly so far, someone was bound to help her out. At least, she hoped so. If she was able to put the awning out, she could set up her folding lounge chair and maybe do some writing outside. That would definitely be different for her.

As she sat at the dining table and looked out the window at the campers around her, once again, she felt she was in a whole other world. It had been over a week already, and Kate could see how this lifestyle would attract people. She still wasn't sold herself, but the relaxed atmosphere where people slowed down to enjoy the moment had a certain appeal. Right now, though, it was time for a phone call to her dad before changing clothes and heading to dinner with the Maddens. She wanted to let him know where she was but more importantly, she wanted to hear his reassuring voice.

"Hey, sweetheart! Where are you?" Martin asked. He didn't even say hello when he answered his phone.

"Hello to you too, Dad," Kate said with a laugh.

"Sorry. Just wanted to put a mark on the map of where you are."

"What map?"

"I've got a map on the wall in my office, and I mark it each time you call or I read where you are. Everyone comes by to check it out and find out how you are doing. Man, I wish I was with you," he said longingly.

"I wish you were too, but we've made plans for Vegas, right?"

They had talked about how her father and possibly his girlfriend would fly out and meet her in Las Vegas for a few days. This was something she was looking forward to—along with her hotel reservation.

"Definitely! Are you doing OK? Met anyone? Made any friends? Met any guys?"

"Dad! Goodness! I've met a lot of really nice people. Actually, people are recognizing me. I'm even having dinner with a nice couple this evening, and they own a few magazines and newspapers. They said they might want to do a story about my trip! That's kinda cool."

"A magazine article about you? That would be fantastic! But what about guys?"

"What are you trying to do? Do you want me to find a boyfriend at a campground?" Kate laughed.

"Well, you never know," Martin said. "Thomas has been asking about you. Has called me every day since you left. I think he's regretting the two of you breaking things off."

"Sorry, Dad, but I'm not. We were only good friends, and I can see that now, especially since I've been gone. He is a sweetheart but just not right for me. I'm sure the perfect guy will come along and sweep me off my feet. You know, like those princesses in fairy tales," Kate said in a sweeping voice that ended in a giggle.

"You might be right."

"Dad, you are truly a romantic at heart."

"I am, but just don't tell anyone. Would ruin my bad boy reputation," he said.

Kate loved her dad, and they were so close. It had been just the two of them for so many years now. Even when she traveled to far-off places, she wanted him to go with her, and sometimes he did. The thought of being gone for six months without him left a small ache inside of her. She would just have to look forward to their reunion in Las Vegas.

"I guess I better go. I've got to get dressed for dinner. One thing is for sure—I'm hardly using the microwave. I've been invited to dinners three times already."

"Just be careful. Not everyone is so friendly, but you already know that from the traveling you have done. I shouldn't be worried, but that's just what parents do when they are concerned about their kids. I love you, girl. Call when you can," her dad said, and they both clicked their phones off.

Kate could feel a small tear in her eye, but she was smiling at the same time. She might not have a mom, but her dad sure made up for it. Right now, she missed him like crazy. But it was almost time for dinner though, and she didn't want to be late.

Nine

"Just in time," Richard said as Kate walked up to the man at the grill. But what caught her eye was the very large motor home behind him.

She stood in awe of the sight before her. Richard and Laurie didn't own a motor home. It was a small moving hotel! It was like something a rock star would travel in. It is *huge,* Kate thought. She was suddenly envious of her new friends but cringed inside when she wondered how anyone could drive such a thing on any highway. It even looked bigger than the city buses back home!

"Hi there!" Laurie said as she popped her head out of the open screen door. "Come on in for a minute. Dinner is almost ready."

Kate walked up to the mansion of a motor home. Its size still mesmerized her. As she did, Kate noticed an elderly lady sitting in a rocking lawn chair under the massive awning that covered the patio. She was doing some kind of yarn work—maybe knitting or crocheting. It was something her mom had tried to teach Kate before her sudden disappearance years ago. Kate wasn't an artsy-craftsy person today because it reminded her too much of her mom.

When Kate walked into the house, as she called it, she felt as if she had stepped into a lovely miniature home. It made her little motor home look like a tent! She gazed at the working television, leather upholstery, and the large room that had a sofa with two chairs. The kitchen had a full-size refrigerator with an actual freezer—something that would be wonderful in her rolling home.

"I just have to grab the salad. If you don't mind getting that stack of plates, utensils, and napkins, we can head outside and have dinner." Laurie was smiling sweetly, and Kate still stood and stared at all the little details of the interior of the large motor home.

"Can I use your restroom real quick?" Kate asked. She just had to see what it looked like, even though it was probably going to make her very jealous.

"Of course. Meet you outside," Laurie said with a smile before walking out the door.

Kate walked toward the back of the motor home, peeking around and admiring everything she saw. As she stepped inside the bathroom, she was dumbstruck. I can turn around without hitting the shower, she thought to herself. And I bet Laurie has never dropped anything in her toilet, Kate thought again. Before heading outside to join the others, she took a quick peek at the room toward the back. She found a large bed, a television that flipped down from the ceiling, tons of storage, and so much more. Kate was brought out of her trance by hearing the calling of her name.

"I'm coming," Kate said quickly, grabbing the plates and utensils before she emerged from the camper to see everyone gathering around the picnic table.

"Kate, this is my mother, Liz," Laurie said, and the older woman sat down in a chair that was pulled up to the head of the picnic table. "She travels with us just about everywhere. Doesn't let any grass grow under her feet."

"Never have and never will," Liz said, and she looked up at Kate. "Very nice to meet you. My daughter has been going on and on this afternoon about something you write on the computer, how you are camping for the first time, and how we have a celebrity coming for dinner. Glad to see you are getting to experience some sites other than what you see on those fancy trips of yours. Nothing like camping, even though Richard and Laurie's camper is nothing like what me and Herbert used to camp in when the kids were little."

"Momma, tent camping is old school. This lets us have a few luxuries while we explore, right?" Laurie said sweetly to her mom.

"Whatever you say," Liz said.

Kate could tell Liz was just agreeing with her daughter to be polite. Kate sensed a tender gentleness in the old woman's eyes. She immediately liked Liz and took the seat beside her.

For Kate, the ensuing dinner tasted like she was eating at a Michelin-starred restaurant. Richard could cook. The steaks were some of the most tender she had ever tasted, and they were cooked over an open grill. Laurie's side dishes of creamed asparagus, roasted red potatoes, and cherry cheesecake were divine. The dinner conversation was wonderful medicine to help with the touch of homesickness she was feeling after talking with her dad.

"Do you crochet, young lady?" Liz asked Kate as they took seats around a small campfire after eating.

The night sky had turned pitch black, and they watched the tiny sparks from the fire float into the air above.

"My mom tried to teach me long ago, but I didn't really get the hang of it," Kate said. She did not elaborate about how it reminded her of her very absent mother, but the older woman was very keen.

"Have you and your momma tried lately?"

"My mom left my dad and me when I was a young girl, so I haven't tried since."

"Then I'm gonna teach ya," Liz said. She got out of her seat and very slowly walked toward a bag full of yarn that was stashed in one of the open compartments along the bottom of the motor home.

"Oh, that's OK. I'm not sure my hands are that coordinated." Kate hoped this would deter Liz, but that was not the case.

"Nonsense, child. I can tell you need something to help you relax. This is better than any pill you could ever take. Plus, you can make things for yourself and others."

"Momma, maybe later. It's getting kind of late, and I'm sure Kate needs to work on her latest blog post." Kate looked at Laurie just as she gave Kate a quick wink.

"Will only take a few minutes. Kate, I'm going to teach you the chain stitch. Simplest thing ever. Then a single crochet stitch. You practice those for a while. You could even make a scarf with just those two stitches." By this time Liz had already found yarn, a crochet hook and was back at her rocking chair, looking at Kate to come and join her.

Kate looked at Liz and as much as she had no desire to learn the craft, she couldn't tell the older lady no. So she grabbed one of the empty chairs and sat beside her.

"Let me say in advance that you will have to be patient with me. My mom never succeeded at teaching me." Maybe it was because she left me, Kate thought.

"Let's get started," Liz said, placing the yarn and hook in Kate's hands. As Liz talked and slowly showed her what to do, Kate could only see the memories of her mother. A pang of hurt spread through her.

"Are you okay?" Liz said softly. "Why ya crying?"

Did she tell Liz the truth or just make up some excuse so she wouldn't have to relive that painful time when her mom abandoned her? Before Kate could decide what to do, Liz had made the decision for her.

"This has something to do with your momma. Tell me what happened." Liz's words to Kate were said with such sweet simplicity that before she knew it, Kate had told the woman the whole story: Kate coming home to an empty house when she was eight years old and finding the note her mother had left behind for her father. When he got home and found out that his wife had left them, he was too numb to react at first. The thing Kate remembered the most was the two of them sitting on the couch, her father wrapping her up in his arms and both of them crying, though her dad only let small tears run down his cheeks.

"I hate to speak ill of your momma but some women just don't understand how to be a momma. Sounds like yours. At least you got a great daddy," Liz said, smiling at Kate. "Maybe learning to crochet might heal some of that pain you have tucked away. And also let you know that not all mommas are like that. Might just have to adopt you little girl," the older woman said as she outstretched her arms to Kate, who reached over and gave her a hug.

"Thanks Liz for listening. And for the crochet lesson. I promise I will practice and hopefully make a scarf," Kate said, the tears now drying and a smile upon her face.

"Momma, aren't you getting a bit tired?" Laurie said as she walked out the camper door toward the two women.

"Yes I am. Kate has learned her two stitches and this old woman is ready to go to bed," Liz said as she stood up slowly and started making her way to the camper.

"And since we're going to San Antonio tomorrow, and so is she, let's stay in the same campground. That way, we can get in another lesson or two."

Kate could very well see that Liz's mind was made up and it was fine with her. She felt she had gained a grandmother tonight and started to heal some painful wounds of her past just by simply talking and a little creative activity.

"You know, that's not a bad idea," Richard said. "Tomorrow, if you want, you can follow me through the Houston traffic since it can get a bit busy. We are staying at a campground right on the edge of San Antonio with bus service to downtown. We love going to the River Walk, and I always visit the Alamo, even though I've been several times. Seems as if I learn something new each time I visit."

"Does it have pull-through campsites?" Kate asked nervously. This seemed to occupy her mind every time a new campground needed to be found.

"Yep, they do. Something I look for because of the size of this rig," Richard said with a smile like he could read Kate's worried mind.

"It looks as if we'll be caravanning!" Laurie said with excitement.

"Caravanning?" Kate looked at her. What did caravanning have to do with camping?

"You know. A caravan. A bunch of campers get together, head in the same direction, and stop at the same sights, cities, and campgrounds. Kinda traveling together like they did back in the Old West. Except we have nice comfy motor homes," Laurie laughed, causing Kate to smile. Kate thought her motor home was more of a wagon than Laurie's rolling home would ever be.

"That would be great. Getting through Houston was already making me quite anxious, but if I can follow you, I think that will help. I don't think I will lose sight of you, that's for sure," Kate said with a smile. "Thanks so much."

"Then tomorrow night I'm gonna teach you another crochet stitch. Maybe even some more girl talk. Right now, though, I'm going to bed." Liz slowly made her way to the motor home steps. Then she looked back at Kate. "For some reason, I feel as if I've gained a sweet granddaughter in you, young lady." She reached for Kate's hand, giving it a squeeze. She then carefully made her way into her motor home.

"Wow, she really likes you," Laurie said once her mother was inside and the door was shut.

"She is really nice. You are so lucky to have her. If you don't mind me asking, how old is she?" Kate asked delicately.

"She just turned ninety a few months ago. Daddy passed away almost two years ago, and she has been living with us ever since. When we decided to make this trip, she wanted to come, so once we park the motor home and extend the sides out, she has her own little bed in the front."

"The sides of what do what?" Kate asked. She was not sure if she heard Laurie's description right.

"The sides of the RV extend out to make the interior larger when we are parked," Richard explained.

So, that's why it seemed as if I was walking into a nicely furnished apartment instead of a camper like mine, Kate thought. Even though my motor home is nice and has everything I need. She looked at the bus again, and sure enough, she saw what they were talking about. Kate didn't know why she hadn't noticed this before.

"Where are you heading after San Antonio?" Laurie asked as they continued to sit under the nighttime sky.

"Well, my readers are insisting...no, begging that I visit Roswell, New Mexico. You know, all the alien stuff. Then I think Carlsbad Caverns is close, and I was advised I just had to visit there too. My readers are doing more trip planning than I am. Maybe that is a good thing right now. Part of me would like to just go back home."

"Why?" Richard asked.

"I guess everything is still just so new. Kinda wishing for my own bed back home, which is strange because I've traveled all over the world. I've just never been gone from home this long," Kate said quietly, and then she suddenly wanted to change the subject.

"I'm so glad I came tonight, though. The dinner was wonderful and actually helped get my mind off everything. And I also enjoyed my crochet lessons."

"No you didn't," Laurie quickly said.

"What do you mean?" Kate asked perplexed.

"I heard your conversation with my momma. I know that must have been very hard telling that story about your momma."

"I admit it was hard to talk about my mom but it was also cathartic too. I haven't really talked about it much over the years. Over time, after she left my dad and I, it was just something that happened and I have moved on. It was just the crocheting that brought back a ton of memories from that period of my life. But your mother was really sweet. And what is really neat is that I actually crocheted," Kate said, proudly holding up a string of yarn with uneven stitches and a little lump on the end that was supposed to be that second stitch Liz had taught her.

"Sorry to hear that," Richard said. "Maybe being out on the road for a while is just the medicine you need to get rid of the stress. Travel and Liz's crocheting are sure to help," he said with a small laugh. "It seems like every person we meet, she is determined to make them masters at crochet, and it doesn't matter if they are a woman or a man. Her heart is in the right place. She used to make and sell so many crocheted items, and she had several women working with her. They used to make blankets for the homeless each year at Christmas. It is truly a love of hers. That compartment she went to for supplies is nothing but yarn we pick up as we travel along the way."

"I have an idea!" Laurie said suddenly. "Why don't we go to Roswell and Carlsbad too, honey? We didn't have anything planned after San Antonio anyway. We talked about Dallas, but Kate's plan sounds so much more fun." Laurie looked at her husband with pleading eyes. Her mouth was shaped into a pout.

"Don't you think you might want to ask Kate first? It is her trip you know."

"I would love the company," Kate said quickly, smiling inside that she wouldn't be alone now that she had made some more new friends.

"I don't see why not, but let's wait till we are ready to leave San Antonio," Richard said.

"Yeah, it's a plan!" Laurie squealed as though the trip was already set in stone.

"Thanks again for such a wonderful dinner and the company. What time do you want to leave in the morning? I just need enough time to unhook everything. Still using my checklist. I'm so afraid I'm going to leave something hooked up and drive away with a cord dragging behind me." Kate was serious, even though she smiled. The checklist she had printed and laminated was a lifesaver when it came to setting up the camper and getting ready to leave.

"Let's depart around ten o'clock. That will put us in Houston after the morning rush hour. It will still be busy but not as bad as it could be."

"I'll see you guys then. Thanks again for such a great evening!" Kate said, and she started a slow walk back to the motor home.

As she unlocked and entered the RV, that feeling of being totally alone settled over her once again even though it was only minutes ago she felt like she now had a circle of camping friends. "This is ridiculous, Kate," she said to herself.

These last years she had had so much time by herself. Why the sudden desire to be home? As she lay on the bed and stared up at the ceiling, she knew it had to be because she was going to be gone for six months. Six months! The conversation she had with her dad the day she left suddenly popped into her mind.

"You know you can do this," her father said.

"I know. But this just feels so different. I can't explain it, Dad. I feel as if this will be the adventure of a lifetime, but I'm truly a fish out of water. I can navigate airports, but driving a motor home is scaring the hell out of me."

"You have practiced. I put you through a bunch of situations, and you did wonderfully. Maybe you're not scared of the motor home but being by yourself. I mean really being by yourself and slowing down for once."

Her father's words struck a chord. "What do you mean?"

"You're always on the go. Never taking the time to just be in the moment and relax. This trip is going to make you do that. You are going to have stretches of time where it's just you and the road. At night, you'll be under the stars—not at some high-dollar hotel. Personally, I think that's what has you on edge."

Lying on the bed now, here in Texas, Kate realized everything her father had said was right. Why was she always running? Well, one thing's for sure, she told herself. I'll have plenty of time to think about it over the next few months.

After lying there for a few moments, Kate noticed that she no longer had that pang of longing for home. Now that she had time to think about it, the months to come would help her find out what she really wanted to do with her life—work, relationships and more. She would have plenty of time to think as she drove, and she'd have the evenings to sit and write. Also, if Liz had any say-so, Kate would gain a new hobby, and then maybe she'd even be able to put a painful part of her past to rest.

Ten

"Thank you, Richard," Kate said over and over to herself as they made their way through the maze of Houston's traffic and interstates.

She hadn't realized how nervous she was until she looked down, once again, to see the knuckles on both hands were almost totally white from the intense grip she had on the steering wheel. She was holding it like a lifesaver. It seemed as if every vehicle that came beside her was way too close. She felt like she was on a bumper car ride at a county fair, trying to avoid being hit—except these vehicles were going so fast that Kate was just trying to keep up. Finally, she could tell they were reaching the city outskirts as the traffic thinned out, and her breathing started to slow down, becoming more relaxed. It was a godsend that she had someone to follow through the huge city. Now, she thought about what she would do once they reached San Antonio. Once she left that campground, there would be no one to guide her through the other larger cities she would encounter around the country unless their little caravan stayed intact. Maybe she would reroute her planned itinerary to avoid them altogether. Take a deep breath, Kate, she told herself, and she tried not to worry about it. Take it one step at a time.

Except for a stop for gas, they made their way straight to the beautiful little campground just on the edge of San Antonio, Texas. Once out of the large city, Kate had enjoyed the drive there, finally starting to feel just a bit more comfortable behind the wheel of Monster—so much so that she decided she would have to come up with a new name for her rolling home. The current one was sounding a bit too harsh. The scenery she traveled through was so different from her hometown, and Kate wished she could have taken more pictures. She did snap a few with her iPhone while rolling down the road. Again, she couldn't help but think of all this beauty she had missed every time she had taken a plane to her destination.

As they checked in to get their reserved campsites, Kate saw indeed that the city bus could take them straight into town. Also, there were restaurants that would deliver which sounded so good to her in case she decided not to go anywhere and no one wanted to cook. If some of her friends could see her now! In a camper, fixing food on the grill and riding public transportation. She would just have to remember to carry her Mace with her. Though her dad had bought her a Taser, which she had a permit to carry concealed, it scared her to even think of using it. All she could envision was getting so scared that she ended up using it on herself by accident. Her dad just wanted to make sure his little girl would be safe while she traveled, and just the thought of him, once again, made Kate smile.

Little did he or Kate know she would be making friends along the way. It seemed each campground she had stayed at so far was like a little relaxed village of friendly people, all there to enjoy being in nature and away from large crowds. They were able to have their own stuff with them instead of lugging suitcases and eating from restaurants for every meal. Kate reflected on these thoughts as she drove to her new campsite, once again taking a deep sigh of relief to see she could pull straight through to the designated spot. Now, she thought, to make sure I lined up with the hookups outside. Today, Kate was also determined to stretch out the awning, especially after seeing Laurie and Richard's extending over the patio last night at dinner. And she would be able to use that outdoor chair she had purchased for the trip. It was tucked away in one of the outside compartments that lined the exterior of the motor home, giving her more storage for her trip. If so, she could take her laptop outside to write and soak in the fact she was already in the middle of Texas. Take that, Bubba, Kate thought again, as her reader that had started this whole camping experience came to mind. But she finally looked out the side mirror and hoped she was parked just right.

The Maddens were parked right beside her in their bus, which made Kate's motor home seem like a Hot Wheels car. Their little caravan, she thought to herself and smiled. As she looked out the door, though, for some reason, she looked around for the VW van. A part of her really was hoping Brandon might have changed his mind and come to San Antonio. He had even mentioned a little campground on the very edge of town and this had to be the one he was referring to, so he knew where it was. Kate quickly erased the thought from her mind. He was a passing friend, one of many she was now sure she would meet along the way.

After everything was hooked up and she had water, electricity, and sewer to her rolling home, Kate looked at the contraption on the side of the motor home: the awning. She had practiced several times at the dealership extending the awning to give her some much-needed shade, but suddenly it looked so complicated. Her mind was drawing a blank on what to do. Frustration was mixing in with all the other emotions surrounding her. Kate pulled the lever to release the awning arm, but nothing was happening. She pulled and pulled. Nothing. She went to the other arm, once again releasing the lever. She pulled. Still nothing. "Argh!" Kate said loudly enough for Richard to hear.

"Need some help?" Kate looked over to see that Richard had just finished all the necessary preparations for his RV.

"I thought that I could remember how to do this. Apparently my memory isn't as good as I imagined."

"You look as though you are about to tear it off the side of that motor home. Something got you a bit upset?" he asked as delicately as he could, and he walked up to help.

"No, just wish I could remember what to do with this thing," Kate said quickly. She continued to tug, pull, and curse, but she wasn't mad at the awning. Just when she thought she was making progress on her camping skills, something like this awning would knock her down a peg or two. This caused her emotions to make her feel like she was on some weird roller coaster. She was excited about where she was, but like before, that feeling of wanting to be home and surrounded by friends and the familiar popped up in her mind. So now she had taken out her frustrations on the poor, defenseless awning, which was only there to make her journey more fun and comfortable.

"Let me help you get this awing out before you beat it up," Richard said with a gentle smile, and Kate realized what she had probably looked like for the last fifteen minutes.

"Here's what you do." Richard told her each step, letting her set the awning up, and the instructions came back to her.

Within five minutes, they were both standing under the awning of her motor home. Kate had a feeling of accomplishment and was gaining a bit of that confidence back. Her motor home looked almost like it belonged next to Richard and Laurie's luxurious bus.

"So, what are the two of you doing?" Kate heard Laurie's voice behind her.

"I just put up the awning! Almost by myself!" Kate said gleefully.

"Well, that's just peachy. I leave all that stuff up to Richard."

"You don't set anything up?" Kate asked her new friend.

Kate heard Richard snicker in the background as Laurie answered her question. "Why, heavens no! That sewer thingy is disgusting, and I pinched my finger on this shade thing, but I do set up the lounge chairs," Laurie said proudly.

Kate suddenly realized how much she could do and felt a bit proud. She was making her way across the country in an RV. Just a few minutes ago, she had wanted to be home, but now she was back to feeling excited about what she could do and where she was. Granted, it was only her fourth state, but she was actually doing what her blog readers had wanted from the moment Bubba wrote his comment.

Boy, were her readers excited! The number of visitors to her blog had increased by 50 percent, and this number was growing a little more each day. Even other bloggers were sharing her story, and that caused more people to visit her blog. They were loving her stories, even though there weren't that many so far. She was even beginning to think of camping travel tips she could share— just like she had before on her fancy excursions. These would just be a tad bit different.

"Are you going to town tonight?" Laurie asked.

"Hadn't really thought about it but now that you mentioned it, I probably won't go till tomorrow morning. Would love to see the Alamo. I've been here before, but I never took the time for a visit to that little piece of history. I definitely want to go to the River Walk because I love it there. But I want to go in the evening. Need to take lots of pictures for my readers. One person told me I should go to a rattlesnake roundup in Sweetwater, but the event has already taken place, thank goodness. Me and snakes? No way! About had a panic attack at the Texas Welcome Center when I saw one in the swamp." At that memory, Kate remembered the strong arms that had kept her from falling that day and Brandon's dazzling eyes.

"Ugh! That sounds horrible!" Laurie said with a look of disgust. She shook her head, and Richard just looked at both women with a big grin on his face.

"Richard, thanks again for the help. I would have been cussing up a storm probably by now if you hadn't come to my rescue. Would you guys like to go to dinner tonight? My treat. We can take a bus into the city, or there is supposedly a wonderful pizza place nearby. They deliver, according to the guy at check-in."

"Pizza sounds good to me," Richard said enthusiastically. "I'm a bit tired, and just relaxing this evening sounds perfect."

"I guess it will do, but I'll have to fix something for Momma. She won't touch pizza, but that won't be a big deal. You order the pizza, and we'll eat at our place so Momma doesn't have to walk much. I need to warn you, though. She has already planned out your next crochet lesson. For some odd reason, she is determined to make you a master crocheter. I think she feels it will help you heal."

"What are you two talking about?" Richard said looking very puzzled.

"Nothing, sweetheart. Just some girl talk."

"No problem," Kate said, and couldn't believe that she was actually looking forward to spending time with Liz. She was such a sweet old lady, and Kate wasn't going to disappoint her. I guess I'll finally learn this craft, Mom, Kate thought, sending the message out to the universe.

Kate's phone began to ring in her pocket. As she pulled it out, she saw Thomas's name on the screen. She rolled her eyes and shoved the device back into her pocket.

"Well, that didn't look too good. You OK?"

"My ex-boyfriend calling. Yet again."

"Oh, man troubles. Honey, I have all day if you need to talk." Laurie was now by her side. She obviously wanted to hear all the sordid details.

Kate sighed. "It's really not anything. We broke up a while back when we realized we were truly just best friends. He seems awfully interested in each part of this trip, though. My dad even said he has been calling him to check on me. Just kinda weird since he didn't call this much when I was at home."

"Men. Can't ever figure them out," Laurie said, but she sweetly kissed her husband on his cheek.

"Well, we can say the same about women!" Richard said.

Kate heard the exchange taking place between the couple before her, but the words weren't registering. What she saw shocked her too much. Kate was smiling and speechless.

"Are you OK?" Laurie asked.

Kate didn't answer. She only watched as the Volkswagen van drove down the paved campground road.

Eleven

"I'm fine," Kate said excitedly. "I think a friend I met in New Orleans is here. At least, it looks like his van."

"Did you say 'his'?" Laurie said with a slight smile.

"I'll be back. I'll order pizza in just a bit."

Kate took off down the road to find where the van was heading. The phone buzzed in her pocket once more, and again she ignored it. She was walking casually but the excitement in her at seeing his van was making it hard for her not to run to seek him out. Wonder why he changed his mind? And how did he find the campground since there were a few others by the city? Even if he did have Internet access and could read her blog, Kate didn't reveal her exact location or what she was doing until after she left a place.

Kate continued to walk down the road, peering from side to side as nonchalantly as she could. Still she saw no van. Had it just been a figment of her imagination? A little disappointment was starting to settle in, but it wasn't for long. There was the van and Brandon beside it. He was setting up his tent. She slowed her walk so she could watch him work, admiring his slow, methodical way of setting up everything. He made it all look so easy. Actually, she just liked watching him!

"Hi there," Brandon said, even though he hadn't even looked in her direction.

Kate stopped in her tracks. "How did you know it was me?" she asked.

"Saw you walking up the road. Couldn't help but see a beautiful girl strolling through a campground." He turned around and flashed the smile that made her melt a bit inside.

His blue eyes and those dimples on his cheeks caused a shiver to ripple through her body. At his compliment, Kate could feel the heat rush to her cheeks yet again.

"What are the odds we would be staying in the same campground once more?" Kate asked. She was really wondering now.

"I figured you would be staying at the nicest campground closest to the city, and there weren't that many actually. Remember, I did also tell you about this one back at the welcome center. I drove through once and saw you struggling with your awning. It looked as if you were about to tear it out of the side of the camper. Then I couldn't help but stay here. In case you needed someone to repair it. Hope that's OK," he said with a little laugh.

"Ha-ha. Well, just as long as you aren't stalking me," Kate said with an impish grin.

"Oh, but I might. You never know."

"I thought you were heading to Galveston for a while. What changed your mind?"

"My plans were never set in stone. I went to Galveston but kept thinking about San Antonio after we talked. So, I packed up and headed here." He just stood there and looked at Kate with a smile on his face.

"We are having pizza tonight for dinner. Would you like to join us?" Kate asked. Please say 'yes', she thought.

"We?"

"Oh, yeah. I met this really nice couple and the woman's elderly mother back in Beaumont. I followed them here today. I think Laurie called it 'caravanning,' and thank goodness. Houston traffic scared the wits out of me."

"That must be that huge bus beside you," Brandon said. He came to stand beside her underneath the shade of the pecan tree. "Are you sure you can trust them?"

Kate thought she heard a deep concern for her in his words. "Most definitely. They're really nice and helpful too. Richard actually saved the awning from my wrath today. I was a bit wound up, and I was taking out my frustrations on the poor thing."

"What's got you so riled up?"

"It's nothing really. So, pizza around six thirty. Sound OK?" she said quickly to change the subject.

"I'll be there," Brandon said with that sexy smile.

* * *

*B*randon watched her walk away back toward her camper. What was it about this particular woman that had completely taken him in? Enough for him to wake up this morning, make the drive to San Antonio, and search three campgrounds till he found her. He had dialed his father's number this morning to tell him that he just couldn't follow through with the plan but never pushed the "send" button. Instead he packed up his gear and got on the road as quickly as he could to catch up with her. She was a sexy woman and one he hadn't quit thinking about since the moment they met in Biloxi.

When his father had called him and asked for a favor, Brandon never dreamed he would be happy to accept. He and his father were not talking much right now, and Brandon almost hadn't taken the call. They needed a break from each other—especially Brandon from his dad. He needed time to digest everything that had happened over the last year. That was why he had decided to travel. Being on the road was helping him heal. However, his father told him an old friend had called just to chat, and then he told Brandon about their ensuing conversation. Brandon had reluctantly agreed to help and gladly accepted the offered money, something he felt his father really owed him after what had happened. He knew he was supposed to watch out for Kate without her knowing, but Brandon hadn't expected to actually like the girl. He had planned to watch her from afar.

He had deviated from the plan and went to Galveston because the feelings Kate had stirred up inside of him were uncomfortable. He didn't want to feel for someone right now. He was being selfish, wanting only time for him. Too much had happened and processing it all was the only thing he wanted to do. But then he met this stunning girl who occupied his mind constantly now.

Thoughts of Kate filled his drive to the city. He had been on the road for over a month. His original plan was to visit the southeast portion of the United States and to stay in Florida for a while. That would be far enough away from his home in Arizona.

Though he could have afforded one of the buses Kate's new friends were traveling in, the van and tent felt more like home. They brought back happier memories of his childhood. At thirty-five, he felt as if he needed to find his roots again after so much upheaval in his life.

So, it was pizza night. It sounded good to him, but he was really looking forward to spending more time with Kate with her fun-loving personality. She was so easy to be with. She was sweet, and he loved teasing her about her city girl ways. Brandon admired that Kate had readily embraced the challenge of a cross-country trip, even if reluctantly. In his circle of friends, he didn't know many women who would do what she was doing—especially when they were used to more luxuries than the motor home provided. Though the two of them had talked, he still had so much he wanted to find out about this fascinating woman. Now he couldn't wait for dinner but first Brandon grabbed his stuff and headed to the bathhouse for a quick shower to look his best for Kate.

* * *

The pizza delivery person arrived with three large boxes, their supper for the evening. Kate sat the dinner on the picnic table, and Laurie grabbed some plates and napkins. Once again, Liz sat in her chair at the head of the table. It was almost like what the matriarch of a family would do, and basically she was the head of this little traveling clan.

"I hope you don't mind, but I asked a friend to join us," Kate said, and she looked around at the three people sitting with her.

"Saw you talking to the hunky man by the VW van. Don't blame you for walking away so quickly this afternoon," Laurie said with a silly grin.

"He is just a friend. We met back in Biloxi and then saw each other again in New Orleans. We actually went on a vampire tour together. He is a really nice guy. He was in Galveston but decided to change his trip plans."

"I wonder why." This time Liz said the words, and she looked at Kate with a mischievous smile.

"Are you sure he's not stalking you? There are some really creepy men out there, Kate. Except this one happens to be super cute," Laurie said.

"Hello, everyone."

At hearing his greeting, everyone at the table turned to see Brandon. Kate cringed a bit, wondering how long he had been standing there and just how much he had heard.

"Everyone, this is Brandon," Kate said, starting to introduce him to the others at the table. But before Kate could say another word, Laurie jumped up, grabbed his arm, led him to the picnic table, and placed him right beside Kate.

"So glad you could join us. I'm Laurie, and this is my husband, Richard," Laurie said. She motioned to her husband, who reached out and shook Brandon's hand. "And this wonderful woman is my sweet momma, Liz."

Brandon nodded his head toward the older woman. "Thanks for letting me crash your dinner. I could eat pizza just about whenever."

"Me too. When she lets me," Richard said quickly, motioning to his wife.

"This is just a treat. We might be on the road, but we can eat healthy. Right, Momma?"

Liz was the only one eating grilled chicken on a salad with a dinner roll. "To each his own," she said and continued to eat her meal. Richard laughed slightly.

The conversation around the table during dinner was light-hearted and fun, each telling stories about camping adventures. Kate didn't really have any stories of her own just yet, so she sat and listened. From the way Brandon talked, she could tell he loved to camp and had many tales to share. They were mostly from his childhood. Richard and Laurie had theirs too, but Liz quietly finished her meal and went back to her crocheting in the rocking lawn chair under the awning.

"So, what are your plans for tomorrow?" Laurie asked Kate. "I'm sure your readers are wondering. At least, it looks that way. I checked your blog a little while ago. These people are really getting into your adventure—and misadventures too."

"Tomorrow it's the Alamo in the morning, since I've never been and then I might go back to the River Walk during the evening. I love it there at night! I promised a full report in my blog over the next few days."

"Where will the next stop on this journey of yours be?" Brandon asked out of the blue.

"I think I'm going to Carlsbad Caverns. I've never been there, and from what I've read, it seems pretty interesting. Not sure how I feel about going nine hundred feet underground, but we shall see," Kate said with a sigh thinking about the journey.

"Oh, let's go too!" Laurie said. She looked at her husband with pleading eyes.

Richard just smiled and said, "We'll see."

"Kate, come here," Liz, said suddenly and so sternly that Kate quickly obeyed the older woman. "Get your chair like last night. Where are your crochet supplies I gave ya?" she said, and she picked up her own bag that contained her current crochet project under construction. "I need to see how you have progressed so far."

"Liz, I'm so sorry but I didn't bring my supplies. Plus, I got so busy today once we arrived at the campground, I didn't practice. Promise though I will try to fit it in tomorrow."

"Does this have anything to do with that young man over there?" Liz said, pointing directly at Brandon as he talked to Richard.

"Well, maybe a little bit. But I'm really glad you convinced me to try crocheting. I think I will eventually get the hang of it. Especially since I have the best teacher around." Kate looked at the older lady to see her smiling broadly.

"Go enjoy some time with that boy. He's a good-looking one and seems to be pretty nice. Just tell him to mind his manners!"

Kate suppressed the giggle that threatened to come out at Liz's remarks about Brandon. "Thanks Liz! We will both be on our best behavior." Once again, Kate reached down and gave the woman a hug then made her way back to the sexy man that made her shiver with delight.

Twelve

"That was really nice of you," Brandon said as they walked to Kate's motor home.

"She has been pretty insistent since I met her. She says it's her duty to teach me to crochet. I don't know why. She is so sweet, and I can't believe she's ninety. Going strong, though. I can barely remember my mom," Kate said wistfully.

"Sorry to hear that," Brandon said. Pain showed in his eyes. Kate wondered why he suddenly looked so sad.

"It's OK. She left my dad and me when I was a little girl. I do remember, though, that she always wanted to teach me to crochet. How weird is that? What about your parents?"

"My mother died about a year ago from cancer. My father and sister live in Arizona. We are each dealing with it in our own ways. Mine by traveling. I took a leave of absence from work and decided I just needed to get away from home and people. Then I ran into you, and I just can't seem to stay away." He smiled at her and it made her heart thump just a bit harder than normal.

Damn, he is cute and sure knows the right things to say, Kate thought. "Finally getting you to talk a bit. Back in New Orleans, you were pretty tight-lipped whenever I asked anything," Kate said, remembering the conversations they'd had.

"Haven't really talked to a lot of people since I decided to take this sabbatical from life for a while. But there's something different about you. You are easy to talk to." At that moment, Brandon felt guilty for not telling her the real reason he was there. At the same time, though, he found himself wanting to be with this girl. Not because he agreed to some arrangement but he genuinely wanted to spend as much time with Kate as he could.

An awkward silence filled the space between them. Kate wasn't sure what to say but had an idea. "Why don't you go to the Alamo with me in the morning? If you want, we can then go back to the River Walk in the evening. Since I'm so easy to talk to, you can unleash your burdens on me. I'm a great listener." Wow, she thought. Did I just ask him on a date like I did in New Orleans? The words just flew from her mouth before Kate could even think about it. She watched him and wondered what he was thinking, but it was only mere seconds before she had an answer.

"I think I'll take you up on that offer. What time do you want to leave in the morning? Or maybe this is a better idea. We can go around lunchtime and just stay there till nightfall to enjoy the city," Brandon said. He was looking at her very expectantly.

Kate liked Brandon's idea even more than her own. "Let's leave around noon. Plenty of time to visit both places."

"Then I say it's a date. I'll see you tomorrow, Kate," Brandon said. For a few seconds he softly looked into her eyes before turning to walk into the black night toward his van and tent. Kate stood there thinking about what it would have been like to kiss the man.

That night, as she sat in the bed and wrote her latest blog, her story for today's post just seemed to flow, even though her day had been busy since leaving Beaumont. With the traffic in Houston, her dad's phone call, dinner, and seeing Brandon again, her day had been like a roller coaster—sudden drops but wonderful highs. She had to admit that it ended on a very nice note. Her readers today would learn of her driving through heavy traffic, making campground friends, and planning her upcoming adventures in the city. It had been a week and a half since Kate began this trip. The entries were becoming easier and more fun. Was she actually enjoying it, even with all the ups and downs she had experienced in such a short time? Kate smiled and said yes as she shut the laptop and put it on the nightstand beside her. Instead of being a little homesick, now she concentrated on the memory of Brandon's handsome face as she drifted to sleep.

Kate woke the next day without an alarm. Once again, the same breakfast smells permeated the interior of her camper, and she loved it. To her, it was the signal of a relaxing morning, even though she had yet to cook outside herself. The microwave was still her best friend, but she was starting to warm up to the idea of possibly using the set of pots and pans she had stashed under the counter. Maybe she would even entertain the thought of cooking for everyone. She did know a few recipes, but it would have to wait. She would cook for herself first and then the others. Then she thought of cooking for just her and Brandon. That thought made her smile. She didn't even know how long he was staying in San Antonio, and she had planned on leaving tomorrow. She wanted to talk to the Maddens first, though. Kate liked the idea of traveling together. Maybe Brandon would like to join their gypsy band. The mere possibility of having him around more made her giddy.

"Hey there," Kate said to Richard. He was sitting at the picnic table as she walked by.

"Hi yourself. Heading to get some coffee? I have some made, if you would like."

"Thanks, but I'm going to get a bit of breakfast too. If there is any left. Waited a bit too late to eat. Got busy doing work. Where are Laurie and Liz?"

"Said they wanted to sleep in this morning, and that's why I'm out here with my iPad reading, checking e-mails, and such. We might be on the road, but business still calls. And I still want to talk to you about that magazine article. I told my editor about your story and they are all set to interview you," Richard said as he was staring at the device in front of him.

"Wow! Thanks so much. Maybe we can set something up after I've been on the road for a few more weeks. More interesting stories to tell by then I'm sure. I've been working myself most of the morning so Brandon and I can go into the city today for the afternoon and evening to do some sight-seeing."

"You and Brandon?" Laurie said as she stepped out of the bus in a long, silky night cover-up. On her, it looked like a stylish dress.

"Just friends, Laurie," Kate said, but she was secretly thinking that if more came from this new friendship, she wouldn't be opposed. "Decided to go into the city around lunch time and stay through the evening instead of coming back and forth to the camper. The Alamo first then on to the River Walk. It is so beautiful at night." Kate looked over at Laurie, who had the silliest grin on her face and was completely engrossed in Kate's itinerary for the day.

"Honey, I know you are a very smart woman. You have to know that man looks as if he could be more than a friend, if you get my drift," Laurie said with a wink.

Kate rolled her eyes. "If that happens, which is very unlikely, I'll let you know. By the way, have you guys decided how long you are going to stay here?"

"Originally we weren't even heading this way. My darling wife wants to follow you, and we really don't have a planned itinerary. If you don't mind some old people tagging along, we might just follow you to Carlsbad," Richard said.

"I would love it. I was thinking about leaving tomorrow, but I looked at the travel time this morning. It looks like a long trip so I might stop along the way."

"Sounds like a perfect plan to me," he said before being practically attacked by his now very awake wife.

"Yeah! This is going to be so much fun! Wait till I tell Momma. She was saying last night you needed more crochet lessons." Laurie squealed into her husband's ear just a bit too loudly.

"Ouch!"

"Sorry!"

Kate watched the couple before her and could see how much they really loved each other. That was what she wanted to find, and in her heart, she knew that special person was out there somewhere.

"Do you have a tentative plan for your trip, Kate?" Richard asked.

"My dad and I mapped out a route before I left, but now that I'm on the road, I'm not sure if I'm going to be that rigid. I do want to go to Roswell—readers' choice. I also want to see White Sands, the Grand Canyon, and Las Vegas. Then it's on to California and more, but that's all I can think about right now."

"Let's go ahead and plan on leaving around nine o'clock tomorrow. We will find a campground along the way. Texas, especially Interstate 10, is one long road," Richard said.

"Sounds great!" Kate said. She was so glad her companions were coming along. Then she heard her stomach rumbling and complaining about no food. "Think I'd better get something to eat. Talk to you guys later!" she said, and she began walking to the campground store.

"Enjoy your date today," Kate heard as she walked away from the couple.

"It's not a date," she said over her shoulder while listening to the giggle behind her.

Kate was so lost in thought that she didn't see the gentleman walking out of the bathhouse just as she walked by. The next thing she knew her cheek met the edge of the door. Hadn't she done the same thing in New Orleans? What was it about her and doors?

"Oh, Kate, I'm so sorry!"

It was Brandon's voice she heard as she held her cheek to help with the sting. "My fault. Wasn't watching where I was going. Can't believe my luck with campground doors. How are you this morning?" Kate said. She wanted to put ice on the throbbing spot on her face, but the man standing in front of her suddenly took away the thoughts of the painful spot left from her encounter with the door.

"A little better than you right now. Let's get some ice for your cheek," he said as he reached for her hand and took her into the store and breakfast area. After asking for a plastic bag, he filled it with ice and was back to Kate in no time. "Hope that feels better. I'm really sorry. Do you still want to go into town today?"

"Of course. This was just a little bump," Kate said. "According to my dad, this is normal for me."

Brandon laughed at the adorable woman sitting beside him. She might have been a fancy resort girl almost two weeks ago, but she was slowly turning into a relaxed, all-American girl living a simpler life, even if temporarily.

"Let's say we leave in a couple of hours. I'll come by and get you. Then we'll take the city bus. That is, if you think you can handle riding in some old, dirty bus again," Brandon said teasingly.

"Yes, the bus is fine. You like picking on me, don't you?"

"Of course not." Brandon laughed. "I'll see you in a little while."

Kate watched him walk away once again. She was really looking forward to spending the day with him, and it wasn't until this moment that she thought of her statement to Laurie this morning. Just friends. If Kate was honest with herself, she could see her and Brandon as more than just friends. She had already met some wonderful people on this journey, but there was one particular person she couldn't get out of her mind—and he was walking toward his tent.

Thirteen

He should be here soon, Kate thought, and she watched the clock. The mark on her cheek had essentially faded. The ice did its magic on the red area where her face had met the door. She checked once more to make sure she had everything she needed for the day in her handbag. Then she heard the knock on the camper door.

"Are you ready for San Antonio?" Brandon looked up at her as she opened the door, and he took her breath away.

"Maybe we should ask if San Antonio is ready for us," Kate said with a big smile.

They took the city bus right to the front of the Alamo. Kate was surprised that this important part of American history was surrounded by the huge city. As she and Brandon walked through the building where the once-famous battle took place, Kate was amazed at the history. Why had she not visited this place before?

"Hard to imagine what took place here so long ago," Brandon said in a solemn voice.

"Sad and hard to imagine that the men were able to put up such a valiant fight. Thank goodness the city has preserved the area so well so others like us can step back into history. Though it is a sad story. The towering buildings surrounding this place tend to hide it. I still keep asking myself why I haven't taken the time to explore this place before now."

"It's the city girl in you. Plus, you love those fancy hotels with their spas and such. That was probably more fun to you than visiting some old, historic building."

"You make me sound very snobby. I'm not that uppity, thank you very much," Kate said, even though Brandon was right. She did like her hotels, limos, and first-class flights. It made her feel like a celebrity, and she had worked so hard to get to that place in her life. Now, only weeks into her forced trip, she was beginning to see another side of life that she wanted to say was much simpler and maybe a bit more fulfilling. But then she looked down at her nails and realized that she could really go for a good manicure and pedicure right now. Kate figured this was a sign that she wasn't quite ready to admit that camping might be just as fun or more so than her first class trips.

"I didn't mean to hurt your feelings. Just kidding with you," Brandon said, looking at her to see her smile.

They walked through the crowd, glancing at the collection of artifacts left behind from the people who had defended this place so long ago.

"That was amazing, and I can't believe how long we were in there. I hate to say this, but I really thought I would walk in and right back out. Just long enough to be able to tell my readers I'd been to the famous Alamo. Being there, though, actually realizing the history, is something I'll never forget. Now for some fun at a place I love—the River Walk!" Kate said excitedly. "And it's just across the street."

"I haven't been here in a while. I was much younger last time, but I do remember the boats filled with people going along the river as we walked through the shops."

"Were you with your parents?" Kate asked softly.

"Yeah. My mom loved this place. We came here a few times when I was a teenager. Of course, I was bored. I wanted to skateboard, bike, and play video games—anything except walk around, shop, and eat. I feel just the opposite now." He glanced at Kate with a look that made her feel like he really wanted to be there with her. His slight smile and twinkling eyes sent her happiness meter to the top of the scale. Kate could feel the heat rising in her cheeks and was sure they must be fiery red. Why oh why did she blush so easily? Soon they were walking through a tiny doorway, and they saw the small river before them. Shops were all around, and one of the boats Brandon had just mentioned went cruising by with passengers aboard.

"So, which way would you like to go?" Kate asked, looking to Brandon.

"Let's head this way and just take our time. We are in no hurry, and we can do whatever we want. Sound like a plan?"

"Perfect!" Kate said, realizing she was completely content just knowing Brandon was by her side. This was something she hadn't felt since this whole thing about traveling the United States by camper had begun.

As they began walking along the river, people moved about, and Brandon now felt positive he had made the right decision yesterday morning. He might have been asked to keep an eye on Kate, but now he found himself wanting to be with her. This was the first time in quite a while that he felt as though he was smiling both inside and out. The pain of losing his mother and then his father's betrayal was still there, but Kate was like a new light that shone in a very dark place. He had known he needed this trip and was glad he had followed his instincts. Maybe he wouldn't be traveling in the opposite direction of the turmoil he had left behind, but now it didn't matter. He loved every minute of watching Kate and seeing both sides of this complex girl. She was the uptown city girl, high heels and all, but in the short time he had known her, he could see bits of an outdoor girl starting to emerge. Tonight was the perfect example.

Kate was dressed in a fitted pink T-shirt that had openings that exposed the delicate skin of her shoulders. Her jeans hugged her curves, but her sandals still had a bit of a heel, which most tourists wouldn't have thought of wearing for a day of sightseeing. Her blond hair was pulled back into a ponytail, revealing the nice curve of her neck and shoulders. Yes, she still was a bit overdressed for the occasion. But from the first time Brandon had seen her till this moment, he could tell she was loosening up a bit. Best of all, Kate made him forget the seeming typhoon swirling around him at the moment.

"Let's take a selfie on the bridge," Kate said. She pointed to the walkway that would take them over to the other side of the small river where more shops and restaurants awaited them. "Should have brought my selfie stick," Kate said once they reached the top of the bridge.

"You really use one of those things?" Brandon said with a laugh.

"Sure. They are great—especially when you are by yourself and need pictures for a blog. And why do you laugh at practically everything I say? I know I'm not that comedic." Kate felt Brandon was teasing her once again, but she just smiled.

"It's just that you are so cute. You are so used to living in a high-class world. What you are experiencing now is how most people enjoy their vacations. When was the last time you just went on a vacation? No fancy hotel. No first-class anything. Just went somewhere for fun. Not because it was free or you needed to write about it."

Kate looked around her. She saw the people eating their dinners at the outdoor cafés, children begging their parents for souvenirs and toys, and the boats full of people enjoying their rides along the river as they passed underneath the very bridge she and Brandon were standing on. He was right. Most of her trips were fun but not vacations.

"You know, you are probably right. And I think I just didn't realize it till these last few days. I can't say I don't miss that lifestyle, but this camping thing is growing on me just a little bit. I like the quietness at night and the friendly people. Oh, the smell of breakfast cooking outside almost every morning is also divine." Kate looked around and continued. "I've been to the River Walk before, but tonight honestly feels like the first time I'm experiencing everything around me. It feels different, and I'm noticing things I haven't before." She knew why it felt this way. She wasn't in a rush like she had been on previous trips. Plus, she was sharing this time with Brandon, someone who was quickly becoming very special to her.

"Whatcha thinking about?" Brandon asked as Kate looked up at him.

This startled her out of her thoughts. "Nothing really. Let's get that selfie," she said quickly.

Since Brandon's arm was longer, he took the pictures with her camera. He took one of the two of them on the top of the bridge, and then he took another at the bottom. This one gave them a background of the river, the boats, and all the activity bustling around them. Brandon also took some pictures of Kate by herself for her blog posts. Soon they found a small Mexican café for dinner, filling up on chips, salsa, nachos, and tacos.

"So, you know about me and why I'm traveling all over. Why are you on this trek of yours?" Kate asked. She was hoping to get Brandon to share more of his story.

You definitely don't want to know part of the reason, Brandon thought as he looked across the table into Kate's sparkling hazel-green eyes. "My parents owned a very large investment business and were venture capitalists. Believe it or not, my mom was the CEO. So, when she passed away, my dad took her place. At the time, I was running several businesses of my own—mostly from my laptop. I design apps and have several websites that really run on their own mostly. I also owned a large store that sold hiking and backpacking equipment. We taught survival lessons and more. I loved it there.

"Not too long after my mom died, my dad made this decision to buy the property where my store was located so the company could build a large office complex. It basically shut down ten businesses, including his own son's, in the blink of an eye. I was so mad, but my dad kept saying it was purely a professional decision. He didn't care that so many people had nowhere to go. He just wanted the land, and he continued to say it was a business decision and nothing personal. So, I helped the people find good locations for their businesses then I sold everything in my store, and I left. I didn't tell anyone, especially my dad, what I was doing except for my twin sister, who is very busy with her own set of two-year-old twins and another baby on the way. I hated to put her in the middle of this thing between my dad and me, but she told me she understood. So, I work on the road, and the businesses are doing fine. It also gives me the freedom to just get away from the situation—and my dad—for a while." Brandon told his story with a very sullen voice and a look of pain in his eyes.

After listening to what he had been through, Kate couldn't imagine what Brandon was feeling. "Wow. And here I've been complaining about having to take this camping trip. It's nothing compared to what you are going through," Kate said quickly, and she knew she was right.

"We are both just experiencing things in our own way. We both are going through challenging circumstances but still standing. I say that's pretty good. But let's change the subject, OK? This might be a bit personal, but I just have to say something. The more time I spend with you, the harder I find it to believe you don't have somebody back home pining for your return."

"I travel too much to have someone special. I was in a relationship, but we broke up a while ago. We realized that, though we cared for each other, we were really just good friends. Now I have this time on my hands to think about what I want from life. Since camping is a completely different way of traveling than I've ever experienced before, it's giving me the time to contemplate life instead of only thinking about the next thing I need to accomplish. I can't believe I'm going to say these words out loud, but I think, just maybe, I might like it. The jury is still out, though. I still have a ways to go on this adventure of mine. Now it's my turn. What about you? A girlfriend?"

"Not right now. We broke up right after my mom passed away. Probably my fault, but she just wanted different things from life than I did. I think she did me a favor the day she decided to break things off. I found out she was already seeing someone else before we called it quits, though." Brandon had a smile on his face, but Kate just stared at him in awe.

"I can't believe everything you've been through! Your mom, your dad, and your girlfriend. I'd want to run away too," Kate said quickly.

"I guess I do sound pretty pathetic," Brandon said, and he flashed a heartwarming smile at Kate.

"No, you don't sound that bad. You've just had a lot to deal with in such a short amount of time. And here I'm complaining about having to camp!"

"You've had your share of difficulties too," Brandon said, and he quickly regretted saying anything. He knew about her mom leaving her and being raised by her dad. He also knew about the ex-boyfriend. He had been given a brief history about Kate when he agreed to keep an eye on her.

"No, just a failed relationship, and my dad raised me because my mom left when I was young." Kate's response let Brandon know she didn't suspect a thing.

"How old were you when your mom left?" Brandon asked, again already knowing the answer.

"I was about eight. One day, she just didn't come home. Dad never told me much back then, and he doesn't talk about it now. He has never remarried, even though I have tried to convince him to give it another shot. He's dating someone right now who might change his mind. He and Cynthia have been together for about five years, and I think he might ask her to marry him. I'm just waiting to see, and I've definitely quit bugging him about it. He is just afraid of getting hurt again, and I can understand. As a little girl, I couldn't quite wrap my head around the idea that a mother would just leave her child. Except Liz gave me some good insight during my first crochet lesson in Beaumont."

"What did she say?" Brandon asked, curious what the older woman could have told Kate to help her heal.

"That some women just weren't meant to be moms. Not that they are bad people, just being a mother isn't in their DNA."

"Well, here is to new beginnings and new friendships," Brandon said. He raised his drink, and Kate followed suit. They clinked glasses and then took sips of their drinks as to seal the deal.

"I have to say," Brandon said, "things are getting better now." Especially since I'm watching over you, he thought. "The online businesses are doing great. I'm developing three new apps right now, and one is almost finished. I like the freedom of working from my laptop. When I get back home, though, I might open the store again. I would like to start a charity for children to get them interested in hiking, camping, and the outdoors instead of always being in front of TVs or video games."

"That sounds like a wonderful idea. Now that I'm starting to experience some of the great outdoors myself, I can see where I probably spend way too much time indoors," Kate said. "Not to change the subject but I do have a question for you, though. How old are you?"

"How old do you think I am?"

"Oh no. I'm not doing that. So?" Kate said expectantly.

Brandon laughed. "I'm thirty-five. Can I ask you the same thing?"

"Take a guess."

"Oh, hell no. I know never to guess a girl's age. Talk about ruining a new friendship."

Kate laughed a little. "I'm thirty but driving the motor home sometimes makes me feel as if I'm eighty by the time I get it parked and set up. But it's getting a bit easier each day with more practice. I don't know how you do it in a tent. I love having electricity. I actually need it to use my computer. Wait. How do you use yours if you just have a tent?" Kate asked.

"I have a solar battery. Works like a charm," Brandon said.

"Really? I never thought about that," Kate said. She was astounded at how many new things she was learning each day. "I will have to include that in a blog post. Maybe you could show me how it works."

"I would be more than happy to," Brandon said, and they stood to leave the restaurant. "How long are you staying in San Antonio?"

"I'm not sure. I was going to talk to Richard tonight. We talked about heading to Carlsbad Caverns in the morning if they went into town today, but I don't know if they did. It will probably be too late to ask when we get back. I didn't realize the time till we just got up to leave."

They started walking along the river. Everything was lit up beautifully under the dark evening sky. It was very romantic, and just looking over at Brandon gave her goose bumps. She suddenly had this picture in her mind of him kissing her among the people and the river, making her feel as if only the two of them existed.

"Kate?"

"What?" The sound of Brandon's voice brought her back to reality.

"Are you ready to head back?"

"Sure," Kate said quickly. She was trying not to concentrate on the image of Brandon's lips on hers, but it just wouldn't go away, even during the bus trip back to the campground.

"Even though I'm not sure when we are leaving town, when we do head toward Carlsbad, we are going to stay the night somewhere along the way. I don't relish an eight-hour trip through Texas tomorrow. I might be getting used to driving Monster, but I still get a bit nervous behind the wheel. Smaller travel times make me feel much better," Kate said.

"You have nicknamed your motor home 'Monster'?" Brandon asked with a grin.

"Yes, well at least that was what I have been calling it because at first that is what it felt like—like I was wrestling with this monster while I was driving then having to set up everything at the campgrounds. Now I need to come up with a nicer nickname since we are starting to get along," Kate said as they stepped off the bus in front of the campground.

"Guess what?" Brandon said as they stood on the sidewalk. "The taxi girl took a city bus again. See how much you've accomplished so far on your journey? Your readers will be amazed," Brandon said, and he slightly brushed her shoulder. This gave Kate that same shiver she had felt earlier in the day.

"Where are you heading from here?" Kate heard herself ask Brandon. The next words were spoken before she even thought. "If you don't have anything planned, why don't you join our little caravan to Carlsbad? Then it's up to visit aliens in Roswell," she said with a nervous laugh, hoping he would agree.

"That actually sounds good. Went to Carlsbad Caverns once, but I don't remember a lot because I was really young. It will be like going for the first time, so we can share it together. Do you think Laurie or Richard will mind?"

"What will you be sharing together?"

The voice came from under the awning of Kate's motor home. As the figure moved closer to them, Kate immediately recognized the man. It was her ex-boyfriend—Thomas.

Fourteen

"What are you doing here? How did you know where I was?" Kate was so shocked to see Thomas standing there that she almost didn't know what to say.

"You didn't answer my question," Thomas said very flatly, and he moved toward her and Brandon. "What are you two going to share?" Thomas's voice sounded cold and mean, which had Kate totally perplexed. This didn't sound like the man she knew back home.

"Kate, I'm going to leave the two of you alone. Let me know if you need anything, OK?" Brandon said. He was looking at Kate to make sure she was OK, and then he gave Thomas a nod.

"She'll be fine. I'll take care of her," Thomas said. He was acting like some kind of hero.

"Thanks, Brandon. I can handle this. I'll see you in the morning," Kate said, and she gave him a reassuring look.

"Talk to you later," he said. He gave Kate one last glance and then turned to walk toward his tent.

"You're dating on your trip? I thought you were just going to take this time to be by yourself," Thomas said as he stared at her indignantly.

Kate was so confused. This wasn't the Thomas she knew, and he had completely caught her off guard. "First of all, if I date or not is none of your business. Thomas, we have been apart for a while now and have continued to be friends. Why are you acting this way? And why are you even here?"

"I read your blog and figured out this is probably where you were. If you remember correctly, I was with you when you and your dad planned out your itinerary. And I have a pretty good memory." Thomas was staring at her, and she could make out his angry features by the light coming from the lamppost. "Then I finally got your dad to confirm it for me. For some reason, every time I asked about you or where you were, he avoided the subject. Maybe it was because of him," Thomas said and pointed down the darkened road where Brandon had walked.

"My dad doesn't even know about Brandon. But it's still none of your business."

"Yes, it is, Kate," Thomas said. His voice suddenly changed to soft and mellow. "I still want you. I want to be with you and for us to be together. You are the only one for me, and that is why I flew out here. To let you know. There is no one like you, and you belong with me."

Kate was now shocked for a second time within a matter of minutes. She and Thomas had already gone down this path, admitting they were just friends. She thought he was on the same page as her.

"Thomas, I'm sorry, but I just don't feel that way. We have already talked about this, and I thought we both came to the same conclusion. You are a really sweet guy, but we can only be friends."

"Please just think about it. Everything we shared and did together. We are like the perfect couple. I know I slipped up once, but it made me realize you are the only woman for me. Just give me another chance, Kate. Please?" Thomas was now looking at her with pleading, desperate eyes.

"Slipped up?" Those were the only words Kate was focused on now.

Thomas's facial expression changed. He realized he had made a mistake, and as he opened his mouth to try to explain, no words came out.

"I'm assuming 'slipped up' means you were seeing or saw someone else while we were dating. Correct me if I'm wrong."

"It was only a couple of times. Teresa made me realize how much I really love you." His words sounded more distraught now, but Kate was slowly getting angry.

"You mean to tell me that you came all the way to Texas to tell me that you love me, even though you were with another woman when we dated? We were still supposed to be such good friends when we broke up. Hell, you even helped me get ready for this trip!" She tried to keep her voice low, but as the words tumbled out, her temper flared.

"I'm sorry. Please. Let's just start over," Thomas said once more.

"First of all, the answer is no. And now that you have admitted this fling, I think our friendship is over too."

"Why? Because of some man you just met?" Now his voice changed, sounding a bit bolder as he was getting louder. "Have you already slept with him?"

"I can't believe you just said that to me. You have the nerve to show up here and make accusations after telling me you had an affair? We are—no—were friends. And I certainly don't have to explain my actions to you—or anyone else for that matter."

"Bet your dad would be interested in your new friend. Maybe you aren't the girl I thought you were."

"Have you lost your mind? You are acting like a two-year-old throwing a temper tantrum. This isn't you, Thomas. I think you better leave now," Kate said. She was trying to keep her cool. This whole situation had her so tense and completely baffled but hurt too by the things Thomas said, what he had admitted and acting totally different than the man she had left back home.

"I don't have anywhere to go!" he protested.

"Guess what? That's not my problem. A bus stops at the front of the campground. Jump on it, and find a hotel. I'm sure there's one close. Then hop on the next plane back home, and have a good life. And, by the way, leave my dad alone. He honestly never liked you anyway. He was only being nice for my sake. I'll have to apologize to him when we talk next because apparently he knew you better than I did." With that, Kate went into the camper and slammed the door.

She didn't turn on any light immediately. She just watched to make sure Thomas left the campground. But he didn't. He continued standing outside her door, knocking on it repeatedly, and yelling at her. Then Kate watched as Richard came outside and told him to shut up and leave or he would call security.

"You can't make me leave. I still need to talk to Kate." Then Thomas turned back toward the motor home. "I'm not leaving till you come out and talk to me Kate!"

She continued to watch the scene unfold outside, Richard telling him one more time to leave. But she didn't want her friends involved in this mess so Kate headed outside once again.

"Thomas, I will only say this one more time. Leave now. Walk down that road and go. I don't care if it is on the bus or a taxi but I want you gone. I don't know what has happened to you but you are not a part of my life now."

"I think you better do what the lady says," Kate heard off to the side. She looked over to see Brandon standing there near Richard.

"This is all your fault," Thomas said starting to walk toward Brandon but Kate stopped him.

"I will call security because this is utterly ridiculous. You are making a fool of yourself, Thomas. Just go back home."

Without a word, Thomas looked at the three people before him then turned on his heel and quickly walked down the lane toward the bus stop. She saw Richard and Brandon watching him as she went to sit at the picnic table. It was only then did she realize that she was shaking from head to toe.

"Thank you, Richard. I'm so sorry for what happened. I had no idea Thomas would be here. The things he said, the way he acted— that is not the person I used to date or used to call my friend." Richard continued to watch Thomas walk down the road but Brandon came to the table and took a seat beside her, sitting very close.

"I've been watching him all evening. We decided to just stay at the campground since we have been here so many times," Richard said. "When I saw him sit in your chair under the awning, I asked if I could help him. Just said his name and that he was waiting for you. Wondered if I knew where you were. I told him I didn't know because I wasn't sure what his intentions were. Loudmouth fella, huh?"

Kate was still upset but couldn't help but laugh at Richard's comment. "Not usually, but he did just get a bit riled up. I can't believe he came here. Brandon, I thought you went back to your camper."

"I only walked about three campsites down. I wanted to make sure you would be fine. When he started yelling, I saw Richard come to help you. I just stayed in the background in case anyone needed help. So, that was the ex-boyfriend."

"In the flesh. Hope he finds his way back to Charleston. He said he wanted me back but then admitted to dating someone else while we were supposedly together."

"Wow!" Richard said, wide eyed.

"Yeah, that's what I'm thinking too," Kate said. Her body was finally starting to relax after the confrontation.

"He's gone. Just saw him get in a taxi. Guess he was too good for the bus, or he didn't have the patience to wait," Richard said, and he looked down the campground lane once more. "I'll watch out tonight. If you need anything else, like if he decides to come back and give you more problems, just let me know. You have my cell number. Call if you need it. As loud as he was, though, I'm sure I would hear anything if he decided to show up again."

"Here is mine," Brandon said, pulling out a business card from his wallet. "Anything, you let me know too."

"Thanks to both of you. I feel as if I have two knights in shining armor for protection," Kate said as she smiled weakly. She knew she had made some genuine friends as she looked at the two men before her—and one of them she definitely wanted to get to know better.

"Richard, since you are here, did you want to head to Carlsbad in the morning or wait another day?" Kate asked, trying to take her mind off the angry man who used to be her friend.

"Tomorrow would be fine. We were going to go into the city, but like I said earlier, we've been so many times. And Laurie has made me promise, I don't know how many times, that we would not make any concrete plans and follow you. Don't tell her, but I was fine with going the moment she asked. Love those old caverns and all that alien stuff at Roswell. Want to leave around ten o'clock? We'll drive a little ways then find a campground by the interstate."

"Sounds great to me. Brandon might join our little group if that's OK. He's still thinking about it," Kate said, looking at him. She was almost willing him with her eyes to say yes.

"I would love to. Like I said earlier, I haven't been to the caves since I was a young boy. Would be nice to go again."

"Yeah! Our caravan is growing. This is going to be so much fun. By the way, Kate, glad you sent that other guy packing. Definitely not your type."

The voice came from the window of the big bus facing Kate's RV. It was Laurie. She had apparently been listening the whole time. Kate just smiled and shook her head.

"Then I guess we will all meet in the morning." With that, Richard said good night.

"I'll see you in the morning too. Are you sure you're going to be OK?" Brandon said, as he and Kate got up from the picnic table. This time he put a hand on the small of her back, and she was sure Brandon could feel her shiver from his touch.

"I will be, but thanks for coming to my rescue," Kate said.

She wanted to give him a kiss on the cheek, but something held her back. So much had already happened tonight. That was probably what it was, but she simply couldn't deny the pull she felt toward this man.

Fifteen

The next morning was exciting for Kate. After the terrible encounter with Thomas the night before, she felt closer to these people she was traveling with. Her campground family was all ready to head out on I-10. They were heading farther west than she had ever traveled by road. In her mind, she imagined they were a group of settlers heading out to find their own piece of the real West. Instead of covered wagons, though, they had RVs. Thank goodness! If she thought camping in a motor home was bad, Kate couldn't imagine how women did this 150 years ago!

Kate was especially delighted every time she looked in her side mirror to see Brandon's VW van following close behind her. It made her smile and practically forget Thomas had shown up last night at her door wanting to make things right. How he could even think they had a chance now was beyond her. As soon as things settled down last night, she thought about calling her dad but decided against it. She just needed to calm down and process what had happened. Knowing her father, he might want to confront Thomas, and Kate didn't want him to say anything. She was sure as soon as Thomas cooled off and thought about everything, he would realize what a fool he had made of himself plus would finally accept that they were just not meant for each other.

Driving this morning gave Kate time to think and admire the scenery. She loved the west Texas countryside that the locals called the Hill Country. It was so different from home. She would find her thoughts wandering at times. In those moments, she wasn't paying attention to the road before her, except when a semi truck would suddenly come by and bring her back to reality. Would she ever get used to those things going by her so fast? Kate always found her hands almost numb from gripping the steering wheel so tightly each time one of the big trucks passed her. But she was proud of herself for doing so well thus far.

Kate watched up ahead, keeping Richard and Laurie's rig in sight, which wasn't hard to do. Richard was leading the charge, and Brandon brought up the rear. Kate almost felt as if she was protected and loved the fact that she wasn't alone on this trip anymore. That little piece of contentment felt amazing, and when she talked to her dad tonight, as she had planned to, she knew he would feel better too. Just knowing she had friends she could count on if she needed them, like the other night when help was necessary during the argument with Thomas, was such a comfort.

Kate had only talked to her dad a few times since leaving, even though each night she wanted to call him. She was doing her best to complete this adventure on her own, so different from the traveling she had done before. At first, she always secretly hoped he would just tell her to come back home. However, the longer she was out on the road, the better she felt, and now that Kate had her little camping family around her, it was so much better.

She followed Richard off the interstate and into the Pilot truck center. This wasn't her first truck stop, but this one seemed a bit busier than the others she had previously visited. She needed to fill up the motor home. It was almost on empty, but each fuel lane looked smaller than the one before. As she watched Richard easily maneuver the big bus right to the gas pump, she felt envious of his skills. Kate had certainly done this before, though, and she could do it again. It was just the fact that the center seemed very busy today. In the side mirror, she could see Brandon following her. He was probably wondering why she kept skipping empty spots. Finally she found that the one on the very end was available, so she wouldn't have to maneuver between the many trucks, cars, and motor homes that seemed to be everywhere and were making her nervous. She eventually parked and got out, standing beside her camper. The hot air felt good on her after being so tense with all the activity, and soon Brandon pulled up beside her.

"Does that thing run on diesel?" he asked, giving her an odd look.

"No. Why?"

"Because that's where you're parked. At a diesel pump."

Kate raced around the side to see she had expertly parked right next to the wrong pump. Her shoulders slumped while her heart sank as she looked around. Why hadn't she noticed that before? Probably because she was too preoccupied with making sure she didn't hit or scrape anyone through the crowded area.

"Do you need some help?" Brandon said as he got out of his van and walked to her.

He was so sweet, and she didn't want to admit defeat, but as she looked around, her nerves got the best of her. "I know I can do this, but for some reason, I feel freaked out. Thank goodness you pointed out the diesel pump. If I had put the wrong fuel in this camper." It was all Kate could say before she reached the driver's door. "I have to get to one of those pumps, but I just feel like I'm going to hit something. This place is just too busy for me"

"I could do it for you, if you like, but I think you'll do just fine. You need to have a little more faith in your skills because you're really doing well," Brandon said with no hesitation.

Kate wanted to take him up on his offer of help but knew this was something she had to do. "I need to do it."

With that, she crawled into the driver's seat and started the engine. She pulled through and ever so slowly made her way into the right spot—but not before beads of sweat came sliding down the sides of her face. Once parked and out of the camper, Brandon was once again by her side. "You did great. I think you might have pissed a few people off. At least it looked that way since they were yelling and giving you the finger as they pulled away, but you did it." Brandon stood there with a smile on his face, but Kate felt horrified.

"Are you serious?"

"Well, you were moving a bit slowly and backing up the RV quite a bit. But, hey, it doesn't matter what they think, right?" He was still smiling to make her feel better.

Or was he getting a good laugh at her expense? Right now, it really didn't matter to her. "Will this ever get any easier?" Kate said, and she put the nozzle into the tank to fill it up with gas.

"You're Kate! That girl who's traveling the States." The woman came from the other side of the pump where a huge truck was being filled with fuel.

Kate and Brandon watched the woman walk toward them so fast and stare at Kate in complete wonderment.

"I can't believe it! I read your blog all the time. Saw where you were in San Antonio. Had no idea we would run into you on the road. This is so exciting!" The woman acted as if she was meeting a movie star, and Kate was flattered but also felt a bit unsettled that so many people were recognizing her.

Instead of shying away, though, she was going to embrace this head on. "It's nice to meet you," Kate said, and she extended her hand to the woman. "Kate Palmer. And your name?"

"Oh my! Missy Tate. I can't believe I'm meeting you. Can I have your autograph? And maybe a selfie on my phone? My friends at home are going to love this."

Kate wasn't sure what to say. She was sure the picture would be on Facebook or other social media outlets and give away her immediate location—something she wasn't too fond of. She didn't want to disappoint the woman, though. "That would be fine, but all I ask is you not post the photo to social media until tomorrow or later. Is that OK?" Kate asked delicately, not wanting to create animosity.

"Of course! I'm just so happy to see you. Are you having fun?" Missy asked. She was suddenly standing right beside Kate and was so close that Kate couldn't get to the gas hose.

"I'll take care of this for you," Brandon said quietly and went around the two women.

"Your blog didn't say anything about someone with you. I thought you were traveling by yourself," Missy said with disappointment in her voice.

"Oh, I am. I met Brandon at a campground." Damn! Kate had said his name before she thought. She looked over at him to see him smiling, giving her a wink.

"A campground romance. How sweet!"

"Oh! No. We're just friends. I've made other new friends along the way too. They are over there filling their rig," Kate said quickly. "We are caravanning."

"That is so neat," Missy said, still not taking her eyes off Kate. "We are heading to Carlsbad Caverns and then to Roswell. The kids want to see all the alien stuff."

"Sounds like so much fun. Hope your family has a wonderful time. Let's get that picture," Kate said. Before she knew it, she was telling Missy good-bye and watching the woman practically fast walk into the huge store.

"Thank you so much for pumping the gas. She was a bit eager. I'm so sorry I mentioned your name," Kate said apologetically.

"Don't worry about it. She probably won't even remember it. Also, you're all filled up and ready to go. Need to get anything from inside?" Brandon said as he pointed to the store.

"I have a few snacks I'm going to get out of the fridge when I turn it back on, so I'm good for now. Don't you have to get gas?"

"I should be fine till we get to Fort Stockton. It's only two and a half hours away."

"I'm ready for a break already, and we have only been traveling for a few hours," Kate said.

"Wanna talk while we drive? I know it's not the safest thing, but it might be kinda fun. Will help pass the time." Brandon looked so cute, especially with the boyish grin he was giving her.

"Sounds good to me. Where's your phone?" Kate said. Brandon handed his phone to her, and she quickly put in her number. "Give me a call when we get out on the road," she said and went in the camper.

She quickly turned the refrigerator back on. This was one thing that had to be turned off when getting gas. She had even made a small sticker, which she placed on the dash to remind her what was on her "When Getting Gas" laminated checklist. She grabbed some string cheese, a few whole-wheat crackers, a bottled water, and apple slices. She put everything around her where things could easily be reached, but this time she also made sure to have her ear buds connected to her cell phone to wait for Brandon's call. Suddenly that trip to Fort Stockton didn't seem too bad.

They weren't on the interstate fifteen minutes before her phone rang. An unfamiliar number popped up on the screen.

"Hello?" Kate said quietly.

"Hi there. Now we can talk about whatever."

It was Brandon, and she was going to make sure to put this number in her contacts right away.

They talked almost the entire way to the campground until they were about ten minutes away from their stop for the night. The time flew by with Brandon. He even talked her through a point when she seemed surrounded by the dreaded semi trucks and her anxiety threatened her sanity. Their conversation was about everything, but Kate found herself talking mostly about Thomas's weird behavior last night and listening to Brandon share stories of his mom. When the campground sign came into view, they said good-bye, but it was only for a few minutes because all the people from their little caravan were soon standing at the counter of the camp store and checking in for the night.

Their three sites were side by side for the first time, and Kate was beyond excited. Brandon would be right next to her. His tent might possibly be right outside her bedroom window. As soon as they were parked, she hopped out, made the connections to the motor home quickly, and even set up the awning. She only pinched her finger once, which was an A-plus in her book. Tonight, they were eating grilled chicken, salad, and dinner rolls. As Kate looked around while sitting in her chair outside, she smiled inside, and she knew a grin was also gracing her face.

She was finally embracing this RV lifestyle. She felt more relaxed than she had in quite a while. She was getting the hang of driving Monster but was still trying to come up with a nicer name for her camper. She knew something would come to her now that she was finally making friends with the vehicle she was calling home for this trip.

"Oh my gosh!" Kate suddenly heard loudly.

She looked to her right and saw Missy, the woman she had met only a few hours ago at the truck stop. "Running into each other again. This is exciting!"

Kate got up to greet Missy. She was not sure what to say. "Didn't want to make this a long travel day. After dinner, it's time to blog. How are you?"

"We stopped early so the kids could swim. When they were younger, camping was easier. Now they are ten and twelve, and it's a bit harder to keep their attention. Should have heard them when we said we would be gone for a month! Thought the roof would cave in on my house," Missy said with a laugh in her voice. "We're parked close. Just a couple spaces down."

"Kate, who's your friend?" Laurie asked politely, walking up to the two women.

Missy didn't give Kate a chance to speak. "I'm Missy Tate. I met Kate back at the truck stop. I recognized her from her blog."

"Me too!" Laurie said.

Kate just stood there and observed the excited exchange between the two women.

"We met in Beaumont, and now we are caravanning to Carlsbad Caverns."

"That's where we're heading too!" squealed Missy.

As Kate watched the women talk, she felt as if she was back in high school watching the head cheerleaders talk with excitement about the quarterback.

"You should have dinner with us tonight," Laurie said.

"No, we couldn't impose. There are four of us, and one includes a growing boy. I think he eats more than the other three of us combined," Missy said and laughed.

"We have plenty. Right, Kate?" Laurie said, finally including her in the conversation.

"We sure do. You should join us."

"And let's talk about you joining our little band of travelers. We are all heading to the same place. Should be fun," Laurie said.

Laurie was definitely the outgoing one! She didn't even know Missy and her family well, but she was already asking them to travel with their group.

"I'll ask Al about dinner and be back in a second."

Kate and Laurie watched the woman walk quickly back to her large travel trailer. Her husband was pulling lawn chairs out of the bed of their pickup truck to put on the patio.

"Laurie, aren't you asking them a bit soon about traveling with us? We didn't even decide about each other till we had dinner together."

"Oh, she's fine. Husband and two kids and all. She could probably use a break—or help for that matter." Laurie laughed and even though Kate didn't have any kids, she knew Laurie was probably right.

"Dinner sounds lovely, and thanks for the invite. What time?" Missy had walked back as fast as she had left.

"We usually eat around six o'clock. Sound good?"

"We'll see ya there but what should I bring?" Missy asked.

"I think we have everything except some drinks," Laurie said.

"I have that taken care of. See ya in a bit," Missy said before walking once more very quickly back to the camper.

"See ya at six, Kate, and tell Brandon for me," Laurie said. She gave Kate a sly wink, and Kate just laughed.

"We are just friends, Laurie," she said emphatically.

"Just keep telling yourself that." Kate walked to the other side of her camper to see Brandon sitting in a low lawn chair with his laptop. "Doing a bit of work?"

"Yep. And I hear we're just friends," Brandon said. He looked up at her with his eyebrows raised.

"Are you implying we aren't? I thought we were," Kate said. At least for now we are just friends, she thought to herself.

"We are certainly friends," Brandon said, smiling up at her.

"Dinner's at six, and we're having more guests."

"Yeah, I heard the entire conversation. Your fan from the truck stop."

"You heard all that?"

"Kinda hard not to. Missy and Laurie are quite, shall we say, boisterous." The grin on his face made her giggle slightly.

"You're right. I just stood there and watched them. But Laurie is a sweetheart, and Missy seems nice too. Haven't met her family, but hopefully our dinner will turn out all right. Can't believe that Laurie has already asked them to travel with us. A little too soon I think."

"I think maybe we should get to know them first but Laurie seems to have pretty good instincts about people."

"I guess we shall see how everyone gets along tonight."

The outdoor dinner was surprisingly nice, even with the addition of their guests. Kate wasn't sure at first. They had nine people now, but they quickly put two picnic tables together, and everyone found a seat. There was more than enough food, and everyone got along so well that each person lost track of time. They all told camping stories that even the kids, twelve-year-old Dana and ten-year-old Ian, seemed to enjoy. Richard, Al, and Brandon all shared technical information about their campers. Kate, Missy, Liz, and Laurie talked but mostly listened to Liz tell stories of her childhood. The kids ended up roasting marshmallows, something Kate had wanted to do ever since she started the trip and saw her first campfire back in Biloxi.

By the end of the evening, the Tates had officially joined their band of RVs traveling to the caverns. They were all leaving at ten o'clock in the morning. That was just enough time to get set up at the campground, eat an early dinner, and then go watch the bats fly out of the caverns at sunset. Even though everyone around her was more than excited about the upcoming event, the thought of thousands of bats flying around her made Kate's skin crawl. All she could imagine was one suddenly flying into her hair or nibbling on her shoulder—or bat poop landing anywhere near or on her. She tried to feign excitement, but someone picked up on her true feelings.

"Doesn't look as if you're a very big fan of bats," Brandon said as they walked slowly back to the campers.

"Could you tell?" Kate said sarcastically. "I can't believe people actually want to sit and watch that spectacle. I'm afraid I'll get bit or something."

Brandon couldn't help but laugh again at this city girl. Kate was learning all about the outdoor life, though, and he loved watching her reactions at each new experience. The more he was around her, the desire to be with her increased. He found himself wanting to know everything about her. Even though they had both come out of relationships not too long ago, he hoped he was reading her body language correctly. He hoped she was feeling the same way about him as he was about her. Now, they were walking slower and closer.

"I don't think you have to worry about getting a bite. Those bats are flying out to get something to eat after sleeping all day. You will probably be the last thing on their minds. I watched it as a kid and thought it was really cool. Then again, when you're young, just about anything like that is the best."

Kate was listening to his words, but she could feel the heat emanating off his body as he stood close to her, and it was sending a prickly sensation all over her skin. Being so close to him was intoxicating.

"If it will make you feel better, I promise to protect you," Brandon said in a very authoritative voice with a mischievous grin. "Just stick close to me tomorrow night."

"Thanks so much for being my protector," Kate said with an overly sweet voice, batting her eyelashes and giving him a smile. "I'll see you in the morning."

"I look forward to it."

With that, Brandon walked to his tent but not before looking back at her one more time.

Sixteen

Now their caravan consisted of four vehicles: the Maddens' big bus, Kate's twenty-five-foot motor home, Brandon's Volkswagen van, and the Tates' dually truck and thirty-two-foot travel trailer. They all had cell phone numbers for each other to be able to communicate while traveling. Kate smiled as she drove, thinking about their growing camping family. This was something she would surely blog about. When she was planning this trip, the idea of forming close friendships had never entered her mind. She especially hadn't thought that one friend might be a very dashing man who was always on her mind.

Today, she and Brandon didn't chat on the phone like they had yesterday. Brandon was doing some conference calls, and Kate had decided it was time for another talk with her father. Hopefully she would be able to catch him at work. She had two hours before they reached their campground near the entrance to the caverns. It was a perfect time to ask her dad about what was going on at home and, most importantly, if he had heard anything about Thomas.

After they were on the road for about fifteen minutes, she dialed her father's number. She knew there was a one-hour time difference, so she kept her fingers crossed she would catch him at lunch.

"Hi there, baby girl," Kate's father said as he answered the phone.

"It's so wonderful to hear your voice, Dad," she said, and she meant every word.

Her father sounded great. At first, though, just hearing his voice brought back a little homesickness, which Kate thought was long gone.

"I've been keeping up with your blog. Looks as if your readers are having a blast following you, and I know I'm certainly enjoying it. I miss you, though. How is everything going? I heard you had a visitor a few nights ago," he said.

"I was wondering if you knew. Thomas is such a jerk. I'm so glad now we called things off," Kate said, reliving some of the memories from that night.

"He said you were pretty mean and that you were with some man."

"He came to see you? And he said I was mean? He was so ugly to me. Thank goodness Richard and Brandon were there with me" Kate said. She was practically yelling into the phone. "Don't believe a word he told you, Dad. That is definitely not how it went."

"I was pretty sure there was another side to this story and I have a tendency to believe my daughter. But is there a man you aren't telling me about?"

Kate then described, in very vivid detail, everything that had happened that night. Her father didn't respond until she was finished with her story. This was mainly because Kate was on a roll and talking nonstop.

"I'm really sorry, sweetheart. I had no idea. He kept bugging me about where you were. I thought he was just being a concerned friend. I guess I got that wrong. But you know how I felt about him from the moment you two started dating. Personally, I think this is a good thing. You now truly know what kind of person he is."

"I agree, but I still can't believe he cheated on me, and I didn't even see it! He could have at least broken up with me and then gone on his merry way. Truthfully, I'm over it. I wasn't as into the relationship as I thought. He was right, though. I have met someone on the road," Kate said very cautiously.

"You have? Who?" her dad said, not sounding a bit concerned.

"His name is Brandon, and he's really nice. Just so you feel a bit comforted, though, I had my Mace with me when I met him," Kate laughed. "But I have developed a lot of new friends lately. The people are so friendly, and some have even recognized me at campgrounds and truck stops from my blog. I never imagined that happening when I left Charleston."

"Just be careful. I don't want anyone taking advantage of my little girl."

"I promise I am. I'm traveling with three families now. Well, two families and Brandon. Anyway, they call it 'caravanning.' I was in Fort Stockton last night, and we plan to be at Carlsbad Caverns tonight. Just in time to see a bunch of bats fly out of the entrance to some hole in the ground. Certainly not my cup of tea, but everyone else seems excited about it. My readers are also heavily encouraging me to go and watch and then walk down into the caverns tomorrow. Dad, just the thought of bats over my head is freaking me out a bit. Plus, I just know there's going to be bat poop everywhere. Ugh!" Kate said, feeling sick to her stomach at the thought.

"Kate, I think you'll be fine," her father said, as he chuckled just a bit.

"You think it's funny, but I think it's gross. Then it's on to alien world."

"What are you talking about?"

"After the caverns, the next stop is Roswell, New Mexico. You know, the alien crash, Area 51—all that UFO cover-up stuff. Another highlight my readers told me I just had to see. To tell you the truth, I'm just ready to get to Vegas so I can stay in a nice hotel. I have reservations for the Bellagio for four nights. I might even extend my stay depending on how long you are going to be there! I will consider it my reward for making it that far," Kate said. She was already thinking of the fluffy bed, big shower and tub, and room service.

"You might miss your camper. You never know."

"I doubt it, but it hasn't been so bad. I've had my share of missteps, that's for sure. Truthfully, though, it's been fun so far. However, I'm keeping that between me and you. Not sure I'm ready to reveal to the world that I might just like this camping stuff."

"No problem there. Hate to do this, but I gotta go. My lunch break is just about up, but I'll let everyone know how well you're doing. I love you, baby girl," her father said sweetly.

"I love you too, Dad. I'll call you when I get to Las Vegas so we can make the arrangements to meet. I can't wait to see you and Cynthia. She is still coming, right?"

"If I get this project finished at work, we have the time off. So we both plan on being there."

"Good! Take care of yourself."

With that, Kate pressed the disconnect button on her earpiece. She had talked to him for twenty minutes, but it felt like only five. She missed her dad and was looking so forward to spending some fun time in Vegas with him and Cynthia. And hopefully Brandon would want to come along if he decided to follow her there. Kate would just have to wait and see.

As she drove along the Texas highway, she wondered if Brandon was free to talk again but she knew he was supposed to be in those meetings. She settled for watching the scenery with a little music in the background. As they got closer to New Mexico, the land seemed to get sparser and flatter. It was totally different from when she had entered this great big state. Before she knew it, a sign appeared welcoming her to New Mexico, and she entered into her next state. Now it was on to face thousands of bats.

Seventeen

As their band of campers filed into the campground near Carlsbad, it was almost comical. They had a huge bus all the way down to a small VW van. They were together, though, and so far everyone seemed to be having fun. Kate had never imagined something like this when she agreed to the wild trip, but she was beginning to have fun. Except the thought of to-night's adventure still had her as nervous as a cat, but she tried to put it out of her mind for now.

They all checked in and once again were lucky enough to get campsites next to each other. As for the trip to the caverns this evening to experience the bat flight, they planned on taking Brandon's van and the Tates' pickup truck. Kate tried to think of anything to keep her from having to go, but any reason she thought of that would let her stay at her motor home just made her seem like a coward. Plus, once again, her readers were chomping at the bit for details of her bat experience. This would be one more adventure to test her ability to try something new and see how brave she could be.

Brandon's camping space was only four places from hers, and that was nice. They were the closest together, and she liked it that way. She thought back to her conversation with her father about how he felt about her relationship with Thomas. He had seen disaster coming, so why had she hung on? Being around Brandon and the feelings he brought up inside her made her realize she had been living in her high-dollar, fancy traveling lifestyle too long, and her relationships had been put on the back burner. She could also see that she had just settled for Thomas, wanting to be in a relationship instead of really finding that special someone to spend her time with. But it took meeting Brandon for Kate to realize this. When she got back from this trip or maybe even before it was finished, Kate was pretty sure she would have to thank Bubba for suggesting this adventure.

"We're almost ready to leave. The two kids are going to ride with us since the seats are so small and we have to get there about an hour before sunset. Everyone else is going in Al's truck. Are you about ready?" Brandon said after she opened the door at the sound of his knock.

The closer it got to leaving for the caverns, the more Kate's stomach was in knots. I still can't believe people actually go to see bats fly out of a cave, she thought. Since the moment she had parked and set up the motor home, she had continued to try to think of ways to get out of her scheduled event tonight but nothing she thought of would work. She would just have to go and say a prayer that panic didn't overtake her.

"Sure. Be there in a second," Kate said, and she reached for her tote bag with her cell phone and camera to capture the event. If she was going through with this, she wanted proof she had been there.

Lena will never believe I actually did this, she thought. Before she stepped out of the door, she saw the umbrella she had stashed close by. She grabbed it and put it in her tote. Maybe she could use it as a shield and a bat poop protector.

The group members climbed into their respective vehicles and headed to the national park. The winding road that led to the caverns was beautiful, and the landscape was like nothing Kate had seen before. It was very desolate but wondrous at the same time. They followed the truck in front of them, and Dana and Ian were sitting on a tiny seat Brandon popped up for the ride. Dana was quiet, but Ian was full of questions. This was also their first visit to the caves, and the little boy was so excited he could hardly sit still. Dana did nothing but look down at her cell phone in total silence.

"You are going to love it," Brandon told Ian. "That's what I've been telling Kate too, but I'm not so sure she shares your enthusiasm."

Kate looked over to Brandon and rolled her eyes.

"You don't like bats? What about caves? They are so cool!" Ian asked.

"Not really."

"Have you ever seen one? I have seen bats before but not in a cave or thousands of them at once flying around. This is going to be great! Why don't you like them?"

Being grilled by a ten-year-old was not helping Kate's nerves. They were just about shot, and she wished she had something to help calm her down. Could it be that she had a bat phobia? Since leaving home, this was the first thing that had her completely petrified—except for driving an RV, of course. But now, after spending as much time as she had behind the wheel, it was starting to grow on her. She was getting used to it—just a little.

"They get stuck in your hair, they bite, and they poop all over you," Kate said to answer Ian's question.

Both Brandon and Ian started laughing, and Kate even heard a small snicker from Dana sitting right behind her.

"What movie have you been watching?" Brandon said. He was still smiling and trying to suppress a laugh.

"It wasn't a movie. It's called YouTube," Kate said defensively, but Brandon was right.

In truth, she had never seen a bat up close and didn't really know what they did. Still, even the pictures she had seen of the creatures gave her the creeps.

As soon as they parked, the park ranger informed them they needed to make their way to the amphitheater soon because the flight would begin shortly. The sun was going down quickly and soon the bats would be on their way.

"We are going to sit in a theater to watch bats?" Kate exclaimed.

"It's an amphitheater—outside," Richard said as they all walked the path toward the giant entrance to one of the largest caves ever found.

The first part of the word had escaped Kate's ears. "I know what an amphitheater is. I just find it kind of odd they have a special place to watch bats," Kate said in her defense.

As they all found seats to watch the "bat flight," as Kate was told the nightly show was called, her cell phone rang. Before she could answer it, though, a ranger was standing in front of their group and he was directly in front of her. "Ma'am, come with me."

"What did I do?" Kate said with a bit of panic in her voice.

"No electronic devices are allowed in the theater area. You will have to leave," the park ranger said.

"I didn't know that," Kate said. She was trying to keep her wits about her as a sudden rush of anxiety came over her. Wait, she thought. Maybe this is a way out of this lunatic event.

"She really didn't know, and we were in a hurry to get here. Actually, she is a bit nervous about this whole thing. Thinks the bats are going to fly into her hair," Brandon said with a hint of a smile at the ranger, who grinned.

"Didn't know about what?" Kate said. She was looking at Brandon with a puzzled face.

"Just turn it and any other electronic device you have off. We'll let it go this time."

"Thanks," Brandon said, and he shook the man's hand.

"You just embarrassed me big time!" Kate said. She was so flustered. Brandon, everyone in their group, and a few others sitting around them were laughing at her expense.

"Well, you can thank me because having an electronic device turned on during the bat's departure can garner you a ticket and a fine."

"You have to be kidding," Kate said, and she rolled her eyes.

"Nope. So, you're welcome." Brandon looked back toward the giant hole, and he totally dismissed Kate's stare.

"But why? And why didn't someone say something when we got here?"

"We talked about it as we walked down here but I think your mind was elsewhere," Brandon said. "As for why the rule, it is because electronics can disturb the bats when they make their way

out of the dark cave after sleeping all day," Brandon said. He still had a hint of a smile from this whole thing.

"Here they come," Ian said excitedly as the first few bats began to fly out of the cave.

They were sweeping up fast and flying so quickly. Kate grabbed her umbrella and had it posed in front of her. Her finger was on the button. At the first sign of attack, the umbrella would fly open.

"An umbrella?" Brandon said. He looked down at her hands and back up to her.

"Just in case."

"Rain? There isn't a cloud in the sky," Brandon said, and he looked above him.

"No. In case the bats come this way," Kate said seriously.

Once again, Brandon couldn't help but laugh at the adorable girl by his side. "Kate, these bats are going to come out of that cave and fly up pretty fast. They won't even come near us."

"I'm not taking any chances."

Just as she said the words, thousands of bats flew out of the cave. Kate watched in amazement as more and more bats came out in intervals. They flew so fast and swept up high in the sky. There were so many, and the sheer amount mesmerized her. After a short time, fewer and fewer came out, and this let them know the show was over. Kate looked down to see she was still gripping the umbrella, but it was not needed.

"Oh my gosh! That was incredible! How many bats do you think that was? When do they come back?" she asked.

"According to the park ranger," Ian said, "there are about two hundred thousand bats in the cave. They come back in the

morning to sleep. We will be able to see them tomorrow when we walk into the cave." The boy was practically jumping up and down with excitement.

"Two hundred thousand!" Kate exclaimed. "Tomorrow we are walking into a cave with thousands of bats? No freakin' way! I heard there's an elevator. That's my ticket down."

"Seriously? The walk is beautiful, and the bats don't fill the whole cave. I promise you'll love it," Brandon said, and he looked so sweetly at her.

Kate sighed as people talked around her about the awesome sight they had just witnessed. They were all making plans to come back tomorrow for a day of walking the cave. The only person who wouldn't be joining them was Liz, and though Kate found the show to be amazing this evening, she was beginning to wonder if she could hang out with Liz tomorrow. Maybe she could get some more crocheting lessons, which she hadn't been practicing like she had promised the older lady. But since she knew she would be coming back, the umbrella would be in her tote—just in case.

* * *

As they parked once again in the cavern parking lot the next morning, Kate got out of Brandon's van very reluctantly. She had her small backpack with her, and in it was the trusty umbrella from the night before. Last night's bat flight show had been amazing and nothing like what she had imagined.

However, now she would be walking under those thousands of bats, and she was sure one might swoop down on her or that a sudden splat of poop would land on her. Just the thought made her gag a little.

"Are you OK?" Laurie said as she looked over at Kate.

"I'm fine. To be honest, though, the thought of walking under those bats today is a bit freaky. It doesn't bother you?"

"Heck no. You won't even see them."

"Really?" Kate said. She couldn't fathom how she wouldn't be able to see the bats because of the sheer number that had flown out of the cave the night before. But the thought of this seemed to pick up her spirits.

"They are so high up, it's hard to see. You might spot a few, but it will be nothing like what you saw exiting the cave last night," Brandon said as he came to stand beside her. Laurie had walked off to find her husband, leaving just her and Brandon alone.

"I know my readers are expecting a full report tonight. I sure hope it is worth the walk down. I guess I'm ready," Kate said, then sighed and looked over at the handsome man beside her.

"Just leave the umbrella in the backpack, OK?" Brandon said and smiled at her.

"I promise, but if I see one of those things flying, you have to promise to cover me," Kate said, kidding with him. Goodness, he looked so cute today that it almost took her mind off of where they were heading.

Kate was told that even though it was pretty warm for late morning, once they reached the bottom of the cave and entered what they called the "Big Room", the temperature would be around sixty degrees. As she looked around at everyone walking toward the cave entrance, people had on long pants and shirts and were carrying jackets. It felt weird to be dressing for cooler temperatures while they were currently walking in the heat but the park ranger told her that she would be thankful for the jacket once they reach the bottom of the cave.

They walked as a group down the very steep winding walkway to the dark cave entrance. It looked like a huge endless hole in the ground. Kate wasn't claustrophobic, but the farther down they went into the cave opening, the more she felt as if she couldn't breathe. Relax, she told herself. If you can sit under thousands of bats, you can certainly walk through this cave. Even though she repeatedly tried to calm herself, those words weren't comforting. She was just glad an elevator would be available to bring them back up to the top once they finished exploring the caverns below. She was also glad Brandon was staying close by her side.

Brandon seemed to be near her at all times although he maintained a slight distance. Kate wandered if he thought any of the same thoughts as she. That maybe they could be more than friends. They had spent much time together, talking and getting to know each other. Out of their little band of campers, it was he that she knew the best and Kate liked that. Even though he would make fun of her and call her a "city girl," Kate knew it was all in jest. He was so helpful and seemed almost like her protector. Last night with the bats coming out of the cave, though he had picked on her, he had also kept her from being kicked out of the amphitheater and given a fine for just having a cell phone on! As they made their way with the rest of their caravan group into the dark cave, Kate stuck close to Brandon's side, and she noticed he didn't move away.

"This is so cool!" Ian said.

He walked from side to side and looked in just about every nook and cranny. Most of all, the little boy was straining his eyes to the ceiling above to see the bats as they walked through the portion of the walkway called the "Bat Cave."

"I don't see any. Where are they?" the little boy asked with disappointment in his voice.

At this, Kate felt brave enough to look above. Sure enough, not a bat was to be found. She found it hard to believe they couldn't see any. She remembered how many of the creatures had swarmed out of the cave the previous night.

"I already told you. You're not able to see them. They are too high up and very well hidden," Al told his disappointed son. "But there are lots of other things as we go deeper in the cave."

"Looks as if you won't be needing that umbrella," Brandon whispered in Kate's ear.

She heard his words, but the feel of his breath on her neck and ear made her flesh tingle. She may have had thought this trip was going to be a "no man zone", but during these last few days, this adorable but ruggedly sexy man had been occupying most of her thoughts.

"I guess I won't. Learn something new every day," Kate said.

She was trying to ease the tension between them, but she looked into his eyes. Suddenly they both realized they were standing still and just looking at each other.

"Are you two coming or not," asked Laurie. "I understand if you want to take your own private tour."

"We're coming," Brandon said, which broke the trance between them.

The walk down toward the bottom of the caverns was beautiful. The trail was steep and narrow at times, and she found herself hanging on to Brandon. He always made sure she was safe, especially in a few slippery spots. The rock formations and pools of water were amazing, but nothing compared to reaching the Big Room.

They were now at the deepest part of the caverns for visitors. Kate couldn't believe the size of the enormous room and the beauty of it all. One of her blog readers had promised she would be amazed, and that person was right on target. She stood for a moment, making a circle and looking in all directions at the wonderful sight.

"This is incredible!" Kate said with excitement for the first time, Brandon standing right beside her, looking in all directions too. But then Kate realized the temperature had dropped and reached into her backpack for the jacket she had brought. "I really didn't think it would be this chilly down here. I wasn't going to bring this but now I'm glad I did," she said as she slid into her light all-weather jacket.

"I'm just glad you listened to me this time."

"What do you mean 'this time'?"

"I've been trying to tell you things about camping and the things we're doing, especially if I have been there before, but you act as if I'm trying to trick you or that I'm making things up," Brandon said.

"You do laugh at my expense a lot, so I'm not always sure if you just like to make fun of me or if you are serious," Kate said, knowing Brandon just liked to give her a hard time.

"You are just so easy to tease and too cute."

"So, you think I'm cute, do you?" Kate asked with a flirty smile.

"Especially last night as you sat there ready to unleash the umbrella should you be attacked," Brandon said. He laughed, and Kate couldn't help but laugh too.

"I didn't know what was going to happen. Give me a break, OK?"

As they looked around, people seemed to be going their separate ways—especially Al and Missy as they tried to keep up with their rambunctious ten-year-old son.

"Looks as if people are going on their own tours around the caverns. Would you like to be my partner?" Brandon said with a charming smile, and he held his arm out like a gentleman.

"I would love to, sir," Kate said, and she wrapped her arm around his.

They started walking the trail around the monstrous room. Kate had never been in a cavern and with each new rock formation they passed, she was fascinated. However, what really had more of her attention was the man walking beside her. He was funny, sweet, and caring, and the icing on the cake was he was so damn sexy. She had to admit to herself that she was mesmerized by the stunning man.

"That looks like a giant penis."

Kate and Brandon couldn't help but hear the unusual statement and looked over to see the Tate's eldest child, Dana, standing in front of a huge rock formation. To say they were both surprised was an understatement.

"What did you say?" Kate asked again. She was not sure if she had heard the girl right.

"It looks like a really big penis."

Yes. Kate had heard right. "Uh…" Kate took a look. She had to admit that Dana's assessment was indeed correct. Now was the perfect time to put Brandon on the spot. "What do you think, Brandon?" Kate said. She was looking at him and doing her best to suppress a giggle.

Brandon looked at Kate and then the younger girl standing beside her. He was totally tongue-tied for the first time since they had met, and Kate was loving every second of it. "Well, I guess. Maybe it might. A little bit. I think I'll leave that to you girls to decide."

"See ya," Dana said, and she casually continued her walk along the path.

"Wow. That came out of nowhere. I didn't even see her standing near us," Brandon said quickly.

Kate, however, was laughing so hard she could barely talk. "You should have seen the look on your face. Priceless! But she is right. I wonder if I should write about the giant penis in my blog post tonight," Kate snickered and stepped back to take a picture.

"I'm sure if you do, your comments will soar to new heights," Brandon said, and he finally laughed along with her. Then he turned around and started laughing even harder.

"What's so funny now?" Kate said. She came to stand beside him and looked in the same direction as he was. Before Brandon uttered a word, she knew what he was going to say.

"I think we might have a sex show of sorts going on down here. Now it seems we have a display of two big boobs," he said.

He was still laughing, but so was Kate. The rocks had indeed formed into the shape of a very well endowed woman.

"I didn't know caverns held such interesting, natural art," Kate said, trying to sound serious but with no luck whatsoever.

"Well, I sure don't remember any of this from my last trip here but I was more like Ian. I couldn't be still and probably only saw something for a second and took off for the next thing along the path. I think I'm liking this trip much better," Brandon said, smiling but with a slower, more sincere voice.

They continued their walk along the route, but it was much quieter now. People were more distanced from each other as they explored different parts of the cave. Kate still couldn't fathom how something so large was underground, but her mind was truthfully more occupied by this hunky man walking by her side. Suddenly it seemed as though there was nothing under her feet. She was falling and trying to reach out for something to grab. A pair of strong arms once again caught her in the middle of falling. As Brandon placed her back on her two feet, she looked up. They were mere inches from each other. The next thing Kate registered was the softness of his lips against hers, and she couldn't help but respond in kind. It was tender and sweet, and when they parted, they held eyes for what seemed hours, though it was only a few seconds.

"Are you OK?" Brandon asked softly. "Seems you slipped in a puddle of water."

"I'm fine. Thanks to you."

"Woo-Hoo! I was wondering when that was going to happen," Laurie said as she and Richard came walking around the corner.

Kate and Brandon quickly backed away from each other, and Kate could feel the redness flooding to her cheeks.

"Oh, honey, don't be embarrassed. He's a looker and also a keeper. Go for it, girl," Laurie said, as she and Richard, who just smiled at the couple, walked by on their own private tour of the cavern.

"Well, that was a bit awkward," Kate said, and she looked around her feeling very self conscious.

"She definitely speaks her mind, but I'm more interested in what you think," Brandon said, taking his hand and placing it gently on Kate's face. He took his other hand and placed it on her waist.

"I know I really liked the kiss," she said softly. "And you have been like a lifesaver for me on more than one occasion. Is the timing right for this?"

Kate was so full of mixed emotions. It was hard. Brandon seemed like the perfect guy, but getting involved with someone while she was traveling concerned her. Just looking at Brandon, though, made her heart beat faster, and part of her knew she wanted this relationship to be much more than a friendship on the road.

"I think you are pretty special, Kate Palmer. Personally, I'm very glad I decided not to stay in Galveston." With that, he gave her another very memorable kiss, this one a little more deeply and then took her hand in his.

They walked the rest of the way along the designated path and stayed close together. Kate could feel the heat from him, and it felt so good. Ever since the first kiss, there was this sensation, this energy, which seemed to pass between them. And Kate liked it.

"Ready to take the elevator up? I don't see anyone else from our group. They could be waiting for us topside or still wandering around here," Brandon said, and he looked in all directions.

"I'm ready. It's beautiful here but a bit chilly and damp. I think I'm ready for some sunshine," Kate said with a smile back at Brandon. He answered her with a small kiss on the tip of her nose.

Everyone was indeed at the snack bar restaurant in the gift shop by the time they took the approximately one-minute elevator ride back to the top of the cavern. Kate had gotten a little claustrophobic on the ride up, and she found herself standing close to Brandon and leaning into him for comfort. He slid his hand around her waist, pulling her more towards him, not backing away at all.

"We were wondering if you two were going to stay down there all day," Al said.

"Or maybe you were just making out in some dark place," Laurie said with a small giggle. "I did pass a few spots that seemed like they would be perfect for a pair of lovebirds."

"Ha-ha," Kate said, and she looked at her friend, begging Laurie with her eyes to not say anything more.

"I'm ready to go back to the campground. At least I can get better cell reception there," Dana said. She was acting as though the beautiful park was just a nuisance. Kate knew she probably would have thought the same thing at Dana's age but she wished she could help the young girl truly know how lucky she was to get to experience such a beautiful sight.

"I think we all have things we would like to do before we head to Roswell tomorrow. Are we cooking out together tonight?" Richard asked.

"I think we're just going to have sandwiches. I'm a bit tired and just want to watch some TV," Missy said. "Why don't we plan something for tomorrow night."

"How about tomorrow night in Roswell, let's grill some chicken at my motor home," Kate said since she had yet to invite anyone to her rolling home.

"That would be great and I will bring my grilling supplies. So, does everyone want to leave at ten o'clock again?" Richard asked, taking the leadership role.

As Kate looked around, her entire camper family seemed so content and relaxed. If people had told her a month ago that she would actually be smiling and having fun during this trip, she would have told them they were nuts. For Kate, though, just the opposite was coming true with each day she spent out on the road with her new friends.

Eighteen

It wasn't long before they were back at the campground. Both kids were in swimsuits before Kate had barely opened the door to her camper. She watched them, especially Ian, because he was totally present in the moment. He soaked in everything around him. I've got to learn to do that too, Kate thought, as she watched the little boy run and do a cannonball right into the middle of the pool, splashing everyone nearby.

"What are you going to do now?" Brandon asked as they stood at her camper door.

"I think I'm going to get a snack and write. What about you?" she asked. She wanted so much to ask him to come inside so they could spend more time together.

"I have some work to do. Paperwork, e-mails, phone calls. I've been a little preoccupied these last few days, and I've let my work slip. Maybe we can take a walk around the grounds after nightfall?"

"I'd like that," Kate said, and she watched him walk away as she shut the door.

The day had turned out beautifully, and even though she had visited one the most incredible sights she had seen so far, the high-light of her day was the magical kisses deep in the cavern. Kate could remember every detail and wished so much to feel his lips on hers again. She glanced out her side window to see Brandon setting up a small table with all his work stuff under a type of awning cover attached to his tent. He traveled so simply, and she was still complaining about a too-small bathroom and stubbing her big toe every time she got out of her comfy bed in the back of the motor home. How does he do it? she thought. And why? This was just one of the many things she wanted to find out about this intriguing man.

Kate sat down at the table and started writing her blog. She definitely put in the comment made by her little friend, Dana, but didn't give out any names. She was sure her readers would get a kick out of this and wanted them to experience some of what she was getting to do. Then she sent a quick e-mail and a few attached photos to the dealership to let them know their camper was still intact. After that, she made a few phone calls to some of the sponsors on her site. They were all thrilled with her trip so far, telling her they loved every story she shared. She finished up, ate a microwave dinner—the healthiest she could find at her last grocery stop—and decided to sit outside to watch the evening sunset.

Brandon came around the corner and took a seat at her picnic table. "Feels odd everyone eating separately tonight. Gotten used to our little caravan gatherings."

"Me too. But we have been spending every night together, and today was pretty long. I guess everyone wanted a break, which was fine with me. I was able to get some work done, which I needed to do. How about you?" Kate watched Brandon sitting across from her, unable to shake the blissful feeling she had every time he was around.

"Same here. Work done, and now I can go on that walk with a pretty girl in the camper next to me."

"Which camper?"

Brandon grinned at her. "At the moment, I'm trying to decide. First, there's you. Very beautiful, if I may add. On the other side of my van is a motor home being shared by two elderly gentlemen who are taking their first cross-country trip. One is a widower, and the other is divorced. So, I guess I must be talking about you."

Kate smiled. She could feel happiness welling up inside her. Just looking at this man made her giddy. As weird as it might have seemed to her, it was an emotional high she had never experienced before. A thought suddenly occurred to her: had she not taken this trip, they might have never met.

"It's a little desolate out here, but the sunset is pretty, and we can just walk," Brandon said softly.

As they strolled around the campground, they couldn't help but notice all the different kinds of people and campers. Brandon did his best to explain the various types of RVs to Kate, but she was hardly listening. She wanted to know more about him—not the other people around her.

"So, we head to Roswell tomorrow. Have you ever been?" Brandon asked.

"No. To tell you the truth, I thought it was all just a myth. Didn't really think the town even existed, but I found out quickly it was real. I've been told to visit the museum there. People say that if I'm not convinced of an alien landing, I'm just not paying attention," Kate said, shaking her head. "Have you been before?"

"Only a long time ago, when I was a little boy. It was the same trip when I saw the caverns for the first time. Aliens fascinated me, so my parents took me since the town was close by. I still think they're out there somewhere."

"Are you talking about aliens? You're kidding, right?"

"Nope. This universe is just too big for us to be the only ones here," Brandon said, and he looked up at the sky.

"Never really thought about it that way before. Then again, I've never really thought about aliens except the ones I've seen in movies. Come to think about it, I did see an alien up close before." Kate said this so seriously that Brandon glanced at her with a weird look. "It was on a movie set a couple of years ago. I was invited to Los Angeles by a friend who was the assistant to the director. The makeup they used was amazing." Kate laughed, and Brandon rolled his eyes.

"Now you're making fun of me."

"Just payback for teasing me about the bats."

"Touché!" Brandon said, and he hung his head.

"Well, we are back at your camper. Thanks for the walk and the talk."

He was standing so close that Kate could swear she could hear his heartbeat. Or was it hers? She looked up into his blue eyes, and suddenly it was as if they were being pushed together. Just as their lips began to touch yet again, they both heard a snicker. They quickly looked around to see Laurie staring out her side window.

"Looks as if you two had a nice walk," she said. Her voice was very animated, even though they couldn't see the details of her face.

"It is quite nice out here. Want to come and join us?" Kate said sarcastically.

"Nah, you guys look quite busy. Have a nice evening," Laurie said with a giggle, and she shut the window curtain.

"I'll see you in the morning," Brandon said, and Kate turned to see him starting to walk away.

Damn, Laurie. It had been the perfect moment.

"See you in the morning." It was all Kate could say as she watched him walk away.

She was going to have to talk to her friend. Kate was really beginning to like Brandon, but Laurie was making it very hard for the two to even have a decent conversation—let alone an enticing kiss.

* * *

The next morning, everyone seemed ready earlier than planned—especially the Tates. Apparently Ian had woken up early because he was excited about seeing Roswell for the first time. The little traveling group headed out around nine o'clock instead of the appointed time of ten. It was only a two-hour trip to the town, and they already had reservations at the campground there. As they had before, they followed one another, and the Maddens led the way. Kate was always reassured when she looked behind her and saw Brandon's VW van following her.

They hadn't been able to talk much this morning. They only walked to the campground store to check out together. He seemed rather quiet, and she hoped that what had happened last night hadn't upset him. Kate had wanted to talk to him as they drove, but she didn't suggest it since Brandon was in such a quiet mood. She wondered if something had happened last night after they had parted ways.

It wasn't long before they were all parked in their designated spots at the Roswell campground, but this time they were scattered all over the site. They were only staying for the night, but they were having dinner at Kate's motor home tonight. She only worried that the grilled chicken that was planned for tonight's dinner would fit on her little grill plus the one at the camp spot. Their band of campers had grown, and making sure everyone had food was a problem. Hopefully the local supermarket would have everything they needed. Kate would just make sure that they would go shopping after they visited the famous UFO museum.

Using the same two vehicles they had the previous days, they all made their way to the very popular tourist attraction that was everything alien. Kate tried to show enthusiasm, but this just wasn't her thing. As they rode through town, though, she was amused at alien paraphernalia that seemed to be everywhere. The streetlamps were alien heads; signs everywhere for businesses had green little aliens on them. They even passed a drink vending machine that had an alien inviting them to quench their thirst. There were flying saucers everywhere too, but the local fast-food restaurant caught her eye. It was shaped like a spacecraft! This was definitely a town that had a story, and they were sticking to it—no matter what.

Ian was in the back seat, and he made sure to point out every little detail as they made their way to the museum. If Kate had wanted to ignore anything alien, there was no way. Ian found every object, so by the time they arrived at the museum, it felt as if an extraterrestrial had already visited them. There came a point when Kate had to just laugh, and she suddenly was glad she had come here. This was definitely a place she would have never seen flying from city to city.

"So, are you excited to see your first real alien?" Brandon said to Kate, but Ian was quick.

"A real one!" he practically screamed.

Somehow, Brandon had forgotten about the excited ten-year-old in the back seat, and he hadn't expected such a loud reaction. "Well, maybe not a real one, but I heard they have lots of documents that could prove a UFO did crash here."

"This is so cool," the boy gushed.

When they were finally parked at the building, he got out of the van so fast and moved like a blur. He was quickly at his parents' sides, jumping up and down to encourage them to hurry. His older sister, Dana, was just the opposite.

"So wish I could have skipped this altogether. Maybe there'll be good cell phone reception inside," she said. She walked with her head down, staring at the screen on her phone.

Kate wondered how the girl didn't run into anything.

"You know, I was asking you that question back in the van," Brandon said, and he came up beside her.

He was close enough that they were touching arms. It would be so easy to reach for his hand, Kate thought, but she didn't want to seem too forward, even though they had already shared several kisses she couldn't forget.

"You mean about the real alien? This is all pretty neat to see, but it's just a way for the locals to make a living off an old legend," Kate said.

"You might not think so after seeing the museum. They have some convincing evidence. You never know," he said, and he held open the door to the building for her.

As the two of them wandered through the museum, Kate once again, had to admit something to herself. She was a bit fascinated by what she saw. Of course, the fake alien display was cute, but the papers and research they had available did make one stop and think. As he had in the caverns, Brandon stayed by her side. This time, though, he talked about the alien information as if he worked there. She loved watching him get so enthusiastic about the subject.

"Why are you staring at me like that?" Brandon said as he looked at her.

"You're really into this stuff, aren't you?"

"When I was a little boy, after my first visit here, I decided I was going to be a UFO hunter. I researched and read everything I could about aliens, UFOs, the military, and more. Any movie that came out featuring any kind of alien, I was there. I was a bit obsessed I guess you could say. Now, though, I just like to keep up with it. Kinda like a hobby. Don't you have anything you really like?"

Kate had to think. Off the top of her head, she couldn't remember ever having something she was that passionate about. She felt embarrassed to answer. "Nothing really. Except travel. Once I started with the travel agency, I talked to all the people I knew about travel, convincing them to book everything and anything with me. Once I started earning free trips, I went whenever I could go. My dad even asked one day why I bothered owning an apartment when I was hardly ever home. And he's really right. As we talk, I now have a house filled with stuff I've brought back from my trips, but it's the memories I love the most. That's why I love writing the blog so much. I get to relive my journeys and help others along the way. And now this," Kate said thoughtfully.

"What do you mean?"

"I'm learning so much—that there's more to this world than what I thought was important. Vampires that used to or still do, roam city streets. Alien towns to be explored, deep giant holes in the ground that are natural beauties, and even tiny rivers that seem to light up a city at night. Campgrounds where I'm meeting some of the most wonderful, friendly people ever. And I'm still just at the beginning of my trip."

"Then think how much you have to look forward to," Brandon said softly, once again giving her that look that could hypnotize her. "I think we've finished the tour," he said softly, not taking his eyes off Kate.

"That's probably a good thing." Kate continued to stare at him, unable to look away. She wanted to kiss Brandon so badly at that moment but there were too many people close by, and they didn't need an audience, even though Kate thought for a moment that she almost didn't care what others thought of an open display of affection. But it was too early in this friendship or relationship with Brandon and Kate didn't know which way to describe what was happening between them. So for now, it would be best just to change the subject.

"I need to run by the grocery store and get some more chicken for tonight. Then let you guys grill it up for dinner." This statement broke the trance between the two of them.

Once again it was back in the van and on to do a bit of shopping. By now, Kate knew it was the norm to be surrounded by aliens in the form of giant graffiti paintings on the store facade and to have a complete section of the store dedicated to nothing but extraterrestrial beings. Kate could only laugh and realize this possible UFO sighting had put this tiny place on the map and drew people from all over. And she was glad she was one of the many tourists who had come by for a visit.

Finally back at the campground, she prepared the chicken for the guys, mainly Richard, to cook on the grill. Since everyone else was supplying the rest of the food, it made it easier. Then she heard the knock at her door.

"Come in," Kate said. She didn't bother to see who it was. She knew it had to be either Laurie or Missy but she was pleasantly surprised to see it was Brandon.

"Came to see if you need any help," he said, and he made his way into the camper. "This is the first time I've seen the inside of your motor home. Quite nice!"

"The dealership was really great to give me a RV that they said would be a good size for me: not too big but enough room

I wouldn't feel cramped for my extended journey around the States."

He came to stand beside her at the kitchen sink, giving her that happy sensation that made her whole body tingle. "Richard is insisting on grilling the chicken. I think he feels he's the grill master king, which is fine with me. I do need to know where your portable grill is, though."

"I think my dad put it in one of the outside compartments." Kate stopped the preparation of the chicken as she looked once again into Brandon's eyes. She suddenly noticed he hadn't shaved in a day or so, and his hair was just a little disheveled. This gave him a very sexy look. Oh boy!

"What's wrong?" Brandon said. He was looking at her perplexed.

"Nothing!" Kate said quickly, trying to look away from the man as nonchalantly as possible. "I just need to get this chicken ready. Thanks for setting up the grill."

"No problem. Anything for you."

With that, Brandon walked out the door and Kate watched every step he made. He was definitely well built. She couldn't get enough of his muscular physique and she watched him walk, dressed in the jeans that fit him oh so well.

She could hear people gathering outside, and she soon had everything ready. Kate brought the chicken out just in time. Both grills looked ready to go. Covered food was already lining the picnic table, and someone had borrowed another table from a neighboring site.

"Give me about twenty minutes, and we will be ready to eat," Richard said. His apron was on, and his tongs were in hand.

Kate handed the plate of chicken to Richard, and she stood for a minute watching everyone. Liz was joining them this evening and had even brought her bag of crocheting. She watched as everyone chatted, laughed, and looked so relaxed. Even Dana looked happy, though she was still glued to her cell phone.

As Kate stood there watching the scene before her, a sensation came across her foot that felt most unusual. It was almost as if someone was tickling her. As she looked down, though, she was so shocked that she felt frozen in place. No sound would come out of her mouth until a blood-curdling scream that had everyone on full alarm. They all stared at Kate. She said nothing to anyone but proceeded to kick her leg and started hopping around, still screaming. The only thing everyone saw was a very large tarantula go flying from Kate and promptly landing on the picnic table, right in the middle of the food. This sent almost everyone running in different directions with a few screams of their own—that was everyone except Ian. He thought the spider was the coolest thing ever and reached for the very large arachnid. Al, however, quickly found something to scoop up the offending creature off the table and put him as far away from the campsite as possible.

"Kate, are you OK?"

She knew Brandon was talking to her but no words would form. She could see Laurie and Missy behind him. She was sitting in a chair and Brandon was examining her foot, but everything felt as if she was in a fog. She could hear voices, but things just weren't registering. Suddenly, though, it was if all her senses came back to her.

"Kate, talk to me. Did you feel a bite or sting? I don't see any marks on your foot or leg." It was Brandon talking.

"I think I'm fine. It just tickled but it was a tarantula! I mean, a giant spider! I heard they were around here—but a tarantula? I thought people were just joking about those things living out here. Where is it now?"

"Well, after you flung him off your foot and onto the picnic table, Al was able to put it far away from the campsite. Thank goodness you didn't step on him."

"I had a tarantula on my foot! A big, hairy spider on my foot!" Kate was still trying to process what had happened just a few minutes before. Then she realized the rest of what Brandon had said. "What do you mean it landed on the table? In our food?" Kate's eyes opened wide. She looked at the table backing away, and then glanced at the ground all around her.

"No, it didn't go in the food. Like I said, Al took care of him." Brandon was trying to reassure her and help her to calm down but her anxiety was on maximum.

"Thank goodness you had flip-flops on. Just watch where you walk. Last time I was out here, I stepped on one. Grossed me out, to say the least, but I had sneakers on," Laurie said casually.

Kate had just been starting to embrace the camping lifestyle, but seeing the large, hairy spider on her foot had her very ready for a hotel—right now. This one incident proved to her she wasn't a camper. A tarantula? For Kate, this was something out of a movie—not a camping trip. She had never camped outside the RV, like in a tent, so maybe this was a common occurrence. Well, not for this gal, Kate thought. Where was the hotel with a huge tub and super fluffy bed? One with no bugs!

"Kate, I promise you are OK. I think you scared him more than he scared you," Brandon said as gently as he could. He could tell she was still a little traumatized and wished he could make it better.

"I had a big-ass spider on my foot! Brandon, that is not normal. That's something you see on TV or in a movie. I didn't realize they roamed so freely out here."

"Then you need to know scorpions are here too. Like Laurie said, make sure to wear shoes at all times. In fact, check your shoes before putting them on because they like dark places."

"Are you saying I have to check my shoes—in my own camper—for spiders and scorpions?" Kate's heart was beating faster now, and she felt on the verge of a panic attack.

"Chicken is done! Let's eat," declared Richard, and everyone seemed to act as if nothing had happened—even though, a few minutes before, a huge spider had landed amongst the food on their table.

Just as I thought I could handle this, Kate thought. *I think I was overestimating my ability.*

"Hey," Brandon said, placing his hand gently on her cheek. "You're going to be fine. This is what this adventure is all about, right?" Brandon said. He wanted to reassure her but couldn't tell if he was helping or hurting the situation because Kate's face was hard to read right now.

"At least it wasn't a rattlesnake," Ian said as he went by her to grab a roll off the table. "We went to a rattlesnake roundup, and it was so cool. I didn't know there were so many around here."

Then the young boy walked off as though his words were just simple talk. They shook Kate to her core. "I can't do this Brandon," she whispered to him.

"What do you mean?"

"This camping thing. I'm just not this kind of girl. I've tried for weeks now."

"And you have done rather well. It was just a little spider."

"A little spider? That thing was the size of my hand," she said a little louder than she had intended, but no one looked her way.

"Think of it this way. Now you know what to look for. I doubt you'll run into another one."

"But what about the scorpions and snakes? This," Kate said, as she gestured around her, "this just isn't me. I'm not an outdoors girl. I've tried and I like it but after what happened tonight? I just don't know."

Brandon could see Kate's eyes getting glassy from tears that threatened to spill forth and that she was still running on the excess adrenaline coursing through her body.

"Let's go for a little walk."

After promising they would be back shortly, Brandon took Kate's hand and led her down the campground's paved driveway. The sun was setting, and the breeze felt good.

"Kate, you can do this. I know that spider scared the hell out of you, but you are strong. Look how far you've come. Look what you've been able to do. And tomorrow we're going sliding on the dunes at White Sands. You're going to love it! Don't give up now." Brandon turned her toward him to gauge her reaction.

She had yet to say a word since they had left the dinner scene at her camper. All she could do was look at the ground. Brandon tenderly cupped Kate's chin, bringing her face up slowly to look at his. Without saying a word, he slid his hand to Kate's cheek.

He placed his other hand around her waist and kissed her tenderly on the lips. Kate hadn't said a word, but her lips felt so good to Brandon. Since she didn't back away, he kissed her more deeply than he had before, and Kate responded in kind.

She knew Brandon was trying to comfort her, but anxiety had taken hold of her, and she was having trouble letting it go. Then Brandon kissed her, and all the stress seemed to melt away. As he pulled back, she found herself leaning into him again. She sought his lips this time, more hungrily than before. They couldn't get enough of each other. It was as though the feelings they had denied since meeting each other that very first day came rushing to the surface, and they were making up for lost time. One kiss followed another.

"Sorry about that," Brandon said softly in her ear as he gently embraced her.

"What are you sorry for?" she answered back. She was just now catching her breath.

"I'm not sure. All I know is I've been waiting to do that for a very long time. You are a very irresistible woman, Kate Palmer, and I'm sure glad I met you in Mississippi."

"I have to admit something. I've been thinking about you quite a bit lately. There's just something about you that has me a bit taken aback. You protect me but tease me. You say you like me, and then I get the feeling you're holding back. And now these kisses," Kate said tenderly as she looked up at him.

Still wrapped in each other's arms, they walked back. Everyone was just about finished eating, but there was still plenty of food for the two of them.

As Kate got her plate of food, Laurie came up behind her. "I see you have a happy glow about you. He seems like an awfully good man, and that's a rare find. You might want to think about keeping him around." With that, Laurie went over to sit by her mother, making sure the older woman was fine.

Laurie was right, Kate thought. She watched Brandon talking with the other guys in their camping caravan. He was special.

Nineteen

The next day, it didn't take long before they were at their next stop: White Sands National Park. Even though Kate was still nervous from her spider encounter the night before, Brandon had helped her calm down to see that she could continue on this journey. His belief in her helped her gain her confidence back. Plus, tonight she would have an extra special blog post that she planned to title "Tarantulas Beware". She had recorded it on her phone as they had made their way from Roswell to White Sands. Now just to put it on the computer.

All the campers and van were lined up at the park entrance. As Kate looked around, she saw some white sand here and there, but as for the giant dunes her blog readers had told her about, they were no where to be seen. Probably isn't much to this park, she told herself but at least she could say she had been there.

After her tarantula incident the night before, Brandon had been more than kind. He checked on her and even went through her motor home, checking nooks and crannies before going to his tent. She voiced her concern about him sleeping on the ground with all the bugs and reptiles, but Brandon reassured her many times over he was safe. He also didn't leave her side until she had stolen a wonderful goodnight kiss, which Kate freely responded to. Each minute they spent together, she felt closer to him in a way she had never felt before. This was totally different from other guys she had dated through the years. It was a feeling that left her very satisfied and extremely happy.

She and Brandon had talked part of the way on their trip from Roswell to the national park. It was a two-and-a-half-hour trip on a county road—not like the interstates they had been traveling on so far. It wasn't as bad as Kate had anticipated, though. She actually loved the land they were traveling through. She still marveled over how different it was from her beloved hometown. Talking to Brandon also made the drive more fun.

Their highway conversation was just as varied as before, but it seemed they always found out just a little more about each other. They even learned their fathers had attended the same college in Florida. That shocked Kate, but Brandon didn't seem so surprised. Then they started talking about their high school experiences, and before she knew it, they were ready to explore the newest stop on her trip.

As the little caravan made its way down the winding road into the park, it wasn't long before Kate saw small white sand dunes. They got larger and taller the farther she went into the park. She couldn't believe their height. If it wasn't for the heat outside, Kate would have sworn she was looking at huge mounds of snow. Even the snowplows that had been used to remove the blowing sand off the road gave the effect of a winter wonderland. But Kate knew the temperature was in the nineties and the sand just gave the illusion of snow. When the caravan came to the parking spot, Kate was in awe of what she saw around them.

"This is incredible." It was all she could say as she got out of the RV and looked around.

Huge white sand dunes were everywhere, and she could see a distant mountain range on the horizon. She immediately spotted Ian. He was already trying to run up a dune, but as steep as they were, he was moving slowly for an energetic boy.

"I was right, huh?" Brandon said as he came to stand beside her, and put his hand on the small of her back. "Pretty cool."

"It's beautiful!" Kate said in response.

"Ian, don't you go over that dune! Stay where I can see you!" Missy shouted to her very excited son, but it wasn't necessary.

He was already rolling down the dune. He was laughing so loud that everyone standing and watching couldn't help but laugh along with him.

"Where are those sleds we got at the store at the park entrance?" Missy said.

Her son came to stand before her. He was fully covered in sand and smiling broadly.

"We have ours," Brandon said, holding up the two sleds he had bought for him and Kate.

The Tate family gathered theirs, but Richard and Laurie had decided they were just going to enjoy the scenery and watch everyone else.

"Ready?" Kate said. She looked at Brandon with excitement in her eyes.

"You know, we have to be careful of the spiders, scor—"

"Stop it," Kate said. "This actually looks like fun, and I don't want you to ruin it."

"Me? Teasing you? Never!" he said and smiled. "Let's go."

The white sand dune they climbed was steeper than Kate anticipated. She was definitely getting a workout under the hot New Mexico sun. Once they reached the top, the sight before her was stunning. The white sand dunes seemed to stretch out for miles. It was no wonder they had been warned not to venture out over the dunes for fear of getting lost. After all, each dune looked identical. They had been told to stay on any trails and not to stray away from each other.

"This is amazing!" she said in awe. She gazed as far as she could into the distance while turning 360 degrees.

"Yes, it is," Brandon said, but when Kate looked at him, he wasn't looking out over the white sand. He was gazing directly at her and before she had time to say anything, he gave her a quick kiss. "Ready to slide?"

"You bet!" Kate said.

She set her blue plastic sled, which resembled a trash can lid, on the powdery sand. Before she knew it, Brandon was beside her. Both of them were sitting on the sleds. Their legs were up, and they were ready to go.

"I'll race you down!" he said and pushed off.

Kate quickly followed and slid down the dune fast, reaching the bottom and tumbling into the sand.

"You OK?" he asked.

As she had come to rest right beside him, he was checking on her, but she was laughing hysterically.

"That was awesome! Let's go again!"

Brandon and Kate forgot about their fellow campers as they made four more trips back up the dunes and down again. Each time they laughed harder than the time before. But the last slide down, they actually ran into each other, ending up in one heap at the bottom of the dune.

"I think we are a little tangled up here," Brandon said, looking at Kate who was lying beneath him.

"A little tangled up feels good," she grinned mischievously at Brandon.

"Well, it probably wouldn't be a big deal if we didn't have several people watching us very intently." Kate then twisted her head to the side to see all their fellow campers watching them.

"Just a small collision. Everyone is fine," Kate yelled out to their audience.

"Yep, ya'll look just fine to me," Laurie said with a laugh. Of all people, Kate knew Laurie would say something about the predicament Kate and Brandon had found themselves in.

"I think it's time for some water and shade," Kate said. She stood and seemed to shake off a few pounds of sand.

"Agreed!" Brandon said. His brown hair looked as if it had been frosted white, and Kate couldn't help but giggle.

"Don't move!"

"Why?" he asked.

"I have to get my camera!"

Kate ran into the motor home and quickly got her phone. She took pictures of Brandon, and then they did selfies. Then Brandon, once again, took a few pictures of her for her blog.

"Send those to me," he said. "I want my own copies."

"Most definitely!" Kate said, and she gave him a quick, sandy kiss on the tip of his nose. "Thanks for so much fun. I really couldn't figure out why everyone wanted me to come here, but this is phenomenal. I just wish it was a tad bit cooler."

"Here is some cold water, sand surfers," Laurie said as she approached the couple. "Richard got some great shots of the two of you. I think you guys had more fun than Ian back there. Missy and Al only went down once, and Dana just sat at the shaded picnic table with her phone. I don't even think there's cell reception out here, but…oh well."

"You should try it, Laurie," Kate said as she happily took the cold water bottle from her friend's hand.

"No way," Laurie said. "I did it once a long time ago, and that was enough for me. But I love this park. It's so out of the way, but I think everyone should come here at least once."

"Now that I've been here, I agree. Brandon was telling me last night it was worth it."

"Was that while you were on your little walk?" Laurie said, and she looked at both of them.

"Actually it was," Brandon said. "Kate was telling me she didn't have what it took to continue on this journey after her encounter with the spider."

"Oh, Kate, you are doing wonderfully. If you need any reassurance, just look at what your readers are saying, and I also think you're doing a fantastic job. You had never done any camping before—much less driven a motor home. What you are doing is a great adventure and very brave. I'm not sure I could do what you have done by yourself. Of course, it doesn't look as if you're alone anymore," Laurie said. She smiled at the couple before her and turned to walk back to her camper.

"One thing is for sure. She certainly isn't shy about expressing her thoughts," Brandon said, and he looked over to see Kate's cheeks a little pink. Whether it was from the sun or Laurie's remark, he wasn't sure.

Laurie was right, though, Brandon thought to himself. Kate wasn't alone and really never had been. She just didn't know it, and he wanted to keep it that way.

After a late lunch, it was back on the road again to make their campground in Las Cruces, which was just a little over an hour away. As Kate sat in the driver's seat, this time listening to some music, happiness swept through her at just the thought of Brandon. Their sledding today had been so much fun, but the longer she sat, the more sand she seemed to feel all over her body. For the first time since starting this trip, Kate actually thought she might use the bathhouse this evening instead of her tiny shower. She simply wasn't sure if her little shower was up to the job of removing all the sand that seemed to cling to her body.

It didn't matter. She had felt like a little kid again today, climbing up the dunes and sliding back down. She and Brandon had raced down the dunes, trying to go faster each time. And also laughing more each slide they took. Though he usually won, he was always waiting for her at the bottom of the dune, usually with a sweet embrace or a quick peck on the cheek. Then there was their intimate collision that Kate just couldn't forget. The feel of

Brandon wrapped around her was enticing and she longed to feel that again.

The sun was setting by the time she had her motor home hooked up. This mundane task brought her back to real life. She was becoming a pro now, but she still had a hard time dealing with or even thinking about the sewer hose. She had to admit it was getting better, though. Brandon was on the other side of the campground in a section designated only for tents. She thought that was ridiculous, but he promised to be over later. Once again, after such a long, fun-filled day, each family was having its own dinner or snacks. The first thing Kate wanted to do was take a shower—hopefully before Brandon arrived. Once she saw herself in the mirror, she couldn't believe what a mess she looked. Even though she had brushed off a good amount of sand, she still could see it everywhere, especially in her hair.

After seeing her reflection in the mirror, Kate made the uncomfortable decision to use the bathhouse for the first time since she began her trip. She quickly grabbed a tote bag and put in the necessary things for her shower: shampoo, conditioner, soap, towels, clothes, and the very necessary flip-flops. She also grabbed a can of bug spray and one of her two cans of Mace. After all, her father insisted she have one with her at all times. At the time, she thought he was just being a bit overprotective, but now she was very glad he had insisted they accompany her on the trip, along with the Taser in the cabinet even though she had felt safe on her journey so far.

She started down the road toward the bathhouse, which was right behind the campground store. Before she had barely started walking, she heard a familiar voice. "I can't believe what I'm see-ing. Kate Palmer is going to the bathhouse." Brandon sounded so simultaneously cute and sarcastic that she didn't know whether to roll her eyes at him or give him a sensuous kiss.

"Ha-ha. Just thought I might be able to clean up a bit more properly after our sandy afternoon. I've been doing OK with my camper shower, but I thought it might be nice to have a bit more room to move around. Plus with the amount of sand I collected on myself today, I didn't want to clog up the shower," Kate said with a smile in her voice.

"What do you have in your arms?" Brandon asked. He laughed as he walked beside her with his own towel and personal stuff. "Is that what I think it is? Raid and Mace? This makes you a double threat, human or insect," he said, and he continued to laugh.

"I'm so glad you find me so humorous. After that tarantula last night, I'm not taking any chances. As far as the Mace, it might be a bit much, but a girl never knows. I'm not sure what to expect in this bathhouse. This is my first time."

"I'll tell you what. I'll take my shower and then sit outside on the table there," he said, and he pointed to a small picnic table not far from the bathhouse entrance. "That way, when you're done, I'll make sure you're safe as you walk back to your camper."

"You're making fun of me again," Kate said, sounding a bit irritated.

"I'm actually being serious. Even though you are so easy to tease. I really believe you're safe, but I'm feeling a little protective of you, Kate, so I personally want to make sure of it."

Kate got that sensation again—that tingly happiness that seemed to spread from her toes to the tip of her head. Even though he was thoroughly covered in sand, he was so cute. There was no way she could stay irritated with him. "Thank you, Brandon," she said and leaned in for a quick hug.

Brandon, however, wanted just a bit more, and he cupped his hands on her sandy face. He brought their lips together with a bit of force but a touch of tenderness also. Kate was so wrapped up in the sensations filling her, and then she heard a can hit the pavement. This brought them both back to reality.

"Glad that was the Raid and not the Mace." Brandon chuckled, and he leaned down to pick it up for her. "I'll be waiting here for you."

With that, he walked into the men's side of the bathhouse. Kate was still in a bit of awe from the mind-blowing kiss, and a smile graced her face. She walked into the large women's area to find restrooms and shower stalls with curtains. As she pulled back one to see the condition of the shower, she was pleasantly surprised. Everything was neat and clean. She did a once-over to check for bugs, namely spiders and scorpions, but she felt confident enough to set the can of Raid down on the bench that was to hold her clothing and personal supplies. The Mace she would keep close.

The shower felt wonderful on her body, and as she looked down, the amount of sand running off her in the streams of water was incredible. It seemed as though she had brought half of White Sands with her. Just thinking of their sledding adventure had Kate smiling all over again. Each day seemed more enjoyable than the next.

It had been weeks now on the road, and Kate could tell she was relaxing more. She enjoyed writing about her adventures and was now sharing camping tips—something she never thought she would ever do. She had been quick to judge this camping thing, and a part of her still yearned for a hotel and room service. There was, however, something about this experience that she still couldn't put into words. Maybe soon she would be able to tell herself and her readers all about this feeling that was growing inside about this adventure of hers.

As she looked in the mirror, her hair was wet, and her pajamas were on. She was also finally sand free. She smiled. If all bathhouses were like this, she might have to take advantage of them. They sure offered more room than her little motor home.

"You look all nice and clean," Brandon said as she walked around the corner. "And in pajamas already too! You are too cute, Kate."

"You look pretty good yourself. And sand free," she said with a laugh as he walked up beside her.

As they began the walk back to her motor home, he put his arm around her waist. Kate responded by walking a bit closer. She loved the feeling of connectedness to Brandon and the sense of electricity that seemed to pass through them each time they were together.

"Thanks again for being my bodyguard. Next time I talk to my dad, I will have to tell him more about this really neat guy I met out on the road. He warned me about meeting strange men out here but he didn't say that I might meet a man like you. I think you would pass his test," Kate said. "Nothing but a gentle-men." As they reached the RV door, she turned to face him.

"I might be a gentleman, but you sure make it difficult when you look and smell the way you do right now." His voice was low and sexy as he took her into his arms, holding her so close.

"Would you like to come in for a bit?" Kate asked, keeping her fingers crossed that the answer would be a "yes".

"I think I better get back to my tent. I need to finish setting up the inside and do a little laptop work. Plus, we have a bit of a ride tomorrow. Want to spend our five-hour trip on the phone again? That always seems to be a great way to pass the time."

"I would love that," Kate said, and she reached up for one more kiss.

It ended up being several intimate embraces before the couple finally said good night, and then Kate watched the handsome man, her man, walk back to his campsite.

Twenty

"I sure hope we're almost there," Kate said to Brandon over the phone.

They had been talking during their trip to Saguaro National Park, which was right outside Tucson, Arizona. This was their stop for the evening. Since the national park was smaller and one you rode through, the caravanning group decided they would drive through before heading to their campground for the evening. From what Kate had read on the Internet, this was a park she really wasn't too excited about. But like before, everyone on her blog said she just had to go.

"It's only a few more miles. Do you want to park your camper and just ride with me?" Brandon asked. "I've been before, and the roads are a little winding. Not that you couldn't do it. But the cacti are really neat to see."

"Honestly, I'm just ready for the campground. I'm actually thinking about taking a swim in the pool. Every time I see Ian and Dana go, I secretly wish I was in there with them," Kate said.

"Why haven't you said anything? Why don't we wait till it's completely dark and then go swimming tonight? Maybe even do some stargazing while we float in the water!"

"That's more like it. We can skip the cacti," Kate said wearily.

"No, you have to go. Just think of all the disappointed readers you'd have if you missed one of their appointed parks on the wonderful agenda they've given you," Brandon laughed.

"Very funny," Kate said as she listened to his voice dripping with sarcasm.

"No, really. The park is completely different than anything you've been to. An abundance of cacti, and some are amazingly tall. I think you're really going to like them. So, are you going to ride with me?"

Why couldn't they just go to the campground, Kate complained silently to herself. "Yes, but just a few pictures, and we're out of there, please?"

"What about everyone else?"

"We could always meet them at the campground. It's not far away from the park," Kate said. She was still hoping to skip this adventure.

"Sounds good. I'll call Richard and let him know our plans."

With that, Brandon hung up, and Kate continued to follow the large RV in front of her. But what was really on her mind was the swim to come that night.

She was able to park her motor home right in front of the gift shop at the entrance to the park. From what she could tell, the park didn't look like much but a very hilly area with a desert terrain.

"Are you ready?" Brandon came up to her, smiling happily.

"Don't you ever get tired of visiting one park after another? I just want to spend more than a few days in one place. I might stay for a whole week at the Grand Canyon. Not just for the sights but just to rest a bit. Even though I'm staying in a hotel in Vegas."

"What?"

"I thought I already told you that. Before I started this trip, I planned to take advantage of some free nights I have available to stay at the Bellagio. Four wonderful nights! The thought of room service and a nice soft bed is divine. I will admit—out loud even—that I'm liking this camping thing, though. Even getting used to ole Monster here," Kate said, and she patted the motor home on the side.

"Still haven't thought of a more loving name for your sweet RV?" Brandon asked.

"I'm still working on it. I'll think of something soon, I'm sure of it."

"Well, let's go see the cacti!"

"If you insist," Kate said. She rolled her eyes as soon as her back was to Brandon.

"I saw that," he said, making Kate quickly turn around. "Just give it a try. Are you starting to get camper burnout just when you said you were having fun?"

"I don't know. I think it's just one of those days," Kate said, and she hopped in the van.

The Maddens had already entered the park, but the Tates had decided to go on to the campground. They told the rest of the group they might come back to the park later so this was the first time they really had all gone their separate ways.

As they began down the one-way, narrow road through the park, Kate was glad she was in the van with Brandon. There was no way she felt she could have driven her motor home along the little road. But she also liked just being with the guy that was behind the wheel.

Kate had to admire the desert landscape around them. Once again, the scenery was nothing like she was used to and it seemed the farther she traveled west, the land changed so much. There were less trees, rocky hillsides and mountains. Plants and definitely creatures that were foreign to her. But she loved it. And as they went around a corner, one of the biggest cacti she had ever seen was suddenly in view.

"Oh my gosh!" This was all she could say as she stared at the Saguaro Cactus in front of her that was at least twenty feet tall. As she began to look around, suddenly they were everywhere, and they all varied in size and shape. "Wow! They are so big. I mean, I've seen them on TV and in movies, but this is completely different. Can we get out to get pictures?" Kate said excitedly.

"Let's go a little further into the park," Brandon said. Then he added a very smart sounding "I told you so" as he looked at her with a very smug grin.

Kate wanted to stick her tongue out at him like a two-year-old, but he was right. She was so glad she had decided not to skip the park. The farther they drove along the winding road, the more the amount of cacti increased. They were too numerous to count. This place was the home of the largest cactus in the United States—the same one that was synonymous with the American Southwest. But there were also plenty of different varieties of cacti covering the ground.

"This is really beautiful. And I'm glad I'm getting to share it with you," Kate said. She impulsively reached over and gave his hand a squeeze. "Thanks for being persistent about coming here. I would have missed this amazing place. When are we going to stop and take pictures?" Kate asked again ready to see these giant plants up close.

"There's a turnoff right up here. We'll park and walk a little bit through the plants. Just have to be careful of the animals and insects. We don't want more airborne spiders," Brandon said, and he tried to suppress a laugh.

"I guess that's one night I'll never live down," Kate said, but she started laughing along with him. His laugh was infectious, and she just couldn't help herself.

They parked and soon were standing out among the giant cacti. Kate snapped one picture after another. She was in awe at the holes in the cacti where small desert animals lived. The whole ecosystem was so different from the humid, swampy South she was used to.

"Brandon, come here. It's selfie time," Kate said. She adjusted the camera as she saw him walk toward her out of the corner of her eye. He looked so good today. His dark hair was still a bit unruly, his tank top showed off those nice arms and his shorts completed his handsome look.

"What?"

"What?" Kate said back quickly.

"You were staring at me."

"No, I wasn't!"

"Yes, you were," Brandon said slowly.

"Let's take this picture," Kate said, a little bit flustered that he had caught her admiring him.

She wanted to change the subject, but just then she heard a very distinct noise that froze her in her tracks. Kate had only heard the sound from shows she had watched on TV but she was almost sure what it was. As she looked at Brandon, she surmised he had heard the same thing.

"Please tell me that's not what I think it is, Brandon," Kate said with a plea in her voice.

"I wish I could, sweetheart, but that is definitely a rattlesnake. Now, where that thing is hiding is another problem altogether. That rattle was pretty loud so please don't move."

"You don't have to worry about that. I'm frozen in place with fear."

This was true. Kate hated snakes and had seen her share of them at home. She had already had one encounter with a snake so far on the trip but at least it had been from a distance. But this rattlesnake sounded like he could be just inches away from them. Why was she finding all the little critters on this trip? A tarantula. Possible scorpions. Now, a rattlesnake? Suddenly though she no longer heard the rattle.

"Did it leave? I don't hear it anymore," Kate said quickly.

"Kate, just stand still. I can see it, and he's about two feet to your left. Coiled up partly under a plant. Seems as if you got just a bit too close. I can't say this enough—please don't move. Let's see what he does."

"Like I said a second ago—I'm not moving. But what if it's a 'she'?"

"What?" Brandon couldn't believe what she had just asked. "You're worried about the gender of the snake? Seriously?"

"I needed to think of something else besides a deadly snake coiled near my feet. And guys always refer to animals as males. They could be females you know."

"Only you would start this conversation with a snake close by your side," Brandon said.

Just then, he watched as the snake began to slowly slither away in the opposite direction of the wonderful, crazy girl he was falling for. He suddenly wondered what she would think if she knew the truth about him and the real reason he was on this camping trip with her. Even though he still was following through with the plan, he was here now because he was falling in love with this incredible woman. Now, Brandon just had to figure out how to tell her the truth about the whole situation.

"OK, I think you're safe. He—or she—has moved down the trail. You can move now, but head this way. I think we might have wandered a bit too far off the path."

Kate looked around her slowly and saw the very large snake making its way over the desert ground. Her breath caught in her throat at first, but then she was astonished as she watched the creature slither away. She suddenly felt a pair of strong arms wrap around her, and she turned quickly to hug Brandon. She didn't realize how tense and scared she was till the adrenaline left her body. She needed reassurance the incident was over.

"Are you OK?" Brandon asked softly.

"Yes. Just shaking a bit and a little weak. I'm glad you were here because I had no idea what to do." Kate couldn't seem to let go of the man in front of her, and he didn't seem to mind.

"Always stay still if you're within a couple of feet of a poisonous snake. Most will just go on their way once they feel the threat, meaning us, has passed. I'm proud of you. You kept your cool."

Even though the heat surrounding them was rather warm, Kate and Brandon didn't know. All that seemed to register in their minds was the feeling of their bodies touching each other at each possible point. The bond and connection between the couple was growing with each passing minute they were together.

"Let's head back to the van," Brandon said tenderly. They unwrapped themselves from each other then Brandon reached for Kate's hand as they walked back to the van, keeping her close to him.

After spending so much time with her, Kate was now special to him. She was one of a kind, and Brandon found himself thinking about her all the time. He secretly wondered about her feelings toward him. The kisses and gentle embraces gave him glimpses into what was possibly going through her mind, but he wanted to know. Especially before she found out the real reason he was part of their RV caravan.

The rest of the trip through the park was beautiful, but the rattlesnake had been the excitement—excitement Kate could have done without. When they got back to the park entrance, Brandon leaned in to give Kate one more tender kiss on the lips. She then got in her camper to follow him down the road. Kate smiled. She loved how it felt to have him give her so much attention, protect her, and even tease her about being a city girl. She secretly liked it. Brandon had more than her attention. He was making his way into her heart.

The campground was just on the outskirts of Tucson, Arizona. By the time she and Brandon arrived, everyone else was set up and enjoying the amenities of the camping oasis. That included the nice pool. Before she knew it, Kate was set up in her camping spot for the evening. There had been talk about maybe staying there for a couple of days because the Tates had family who lived close to town, and Liz just loved the area. With the heat the way it was, though, Kate was ready to make her way north. Her next big stop was the Grand Canyon, and she was planning to stay there for at least four days. She wondered if their little caravan would stay together because she was the only person in the group who had never seen the wondrous sight. She had already decided to take the mule ride to the bottom of the canyon. She had reservations at the campground next to the rim of the canyon, and this was one of the places on her trip schedule she couldn't wait to see. She loved her little camping family, but if only one person—Brandon—could stay on this trip with her, she would be one happy girl.

"You're becoming a pro now," Richard said as he walked up to Kate.

She set her chair under the RV awning. "Probably because I had some great teachers," Kate said with a laugh. "There's no telling what shape I—or this camper—would be in if I hadn't met you guys. Are you still thinking about staying here for a couple of days?"

"Liz sure wants to. She likes the heat better than the cold but stays in the camper. Go figure!" Richard said with a smile. "She also has a friend in Phoenix she wants to visit. What do you and Brandon have planned?"

"Me and Brandon? I'm heading to the Grand Canyon. I already have reservations at the park campground for a few days.

Then I'm heading to Las Vegas for maybe a week. Not sure. As for Brandon, he hasn't told me his plans."

"What about me?" Brandon said as he came around the corner. He was just in time to hear his name.

"Are you planning to stay in town or head north with Kate? We're talking about staying here a couple of days, and I know Missy and Al are because of family in the area."

"I'm from Arizona. I was just tagging along, so I'll probably follow Kate. If that's OK with her."

Kate was so happy to hear those words, but she tried to keep it as casual as possible in her response. "That would be fine," she said, and then she looked to Richard. "Maybe you and Laurie could catch up with us since we'll be there for a few days. The Tates might want to also."

"I'll run it by them. What are you doing for dinner?" Richard asked.

"I was just getting ready to ask Kate out for dinner," Brandon said.

"I was wondering when you were going to ask this girl out on a proper date," Richard said, and he gave Brandon a friendly slap on the back. "There's some good eating around here, so enjoy yourselves. I'll let you know before you leave in the morning what we plan to do. Have a great time, you two!"

"Out to dinner?" Kate asked, as she was looking at Brandon with one eyebrow raised.

"Yes. Kate, would you like to have dinner with me? Then maybe we can come back here and take a nighttime swim like we talked about earlier."

Kate's heart was beating so fast, and she was willing it to slow down. "When should I be ready?"

"How about I pick you up in about an hour?"

"Sounds perfect," Kate answered.

She gave her date a kiss on the cheek before going into her motor home to get ready. Since she had a real date, she was going to wear her high heels.

Twenty-One

"So, where are we going?" Kate asked as soon as they turned on the highway out of the campground.

"What sounds good to you? There are a bunch of restaurants not too far from here, so I thought I'd let you choose," Brandon said. He was looking over at her with the smile that made her almost feel breathless.

"Um, let's see. I like Italian, Mexican, Japanese. Well, really I like it all. What about you?"

"Since we're in the Southwest, how about a little Mexican?"

"Wonderful!"

It wasn't long before they were seated in a beautiful, small Mexican restaurant. Kate was in love with the tiny place before they even had their food. She felt as if she had traveled to Mexico, and it reminded her of a restaurant where she had eaten in Cancun.

"I hope it's good. I'm starving," Kate said while looking over the menu.

"Oh, it's good."

"How do you know?"

"I've been here before."

"Really?"

"I used to come here whenever I visited this part of town. My parents have properties in the city. Actually very close to here and that is how I knew about the pick of places to eat." Brandon took a sip of water and just smiled back at Kate.

"Well, aren't you full of surprises?" Kate said with a smile.

If only you knew, Kate, you probably wouldn't be so happy, Brandon thought. He only had a moment to think this, though, before the waiter came and took their dinner orders.

"I know this is our first official date, but I feel as if I know you so well. Except little things. Like, where are you from? I know you're from Arizona. But what city?" Kate said.

"A town outside of Phoenix called Glendale. Born and raised there."

"I can't imagine living in the desert. I'm so used to lots of trees, marshes and high humidity. Plus, I'm such a beach girl at heart."

"Well, that was where I was headed till I met you," Brandon said. "I was going to spend a few months in Florida. I've only been a couple of times when I went to Disney World when I was younger. But I guess plans change. I don't mind this change, though. It's turning out to be one of my best decisions so far." Brandon took a sip of his drink but looked at Kate with a sparkle in his eye.

"Florida is actually where my trip is supposed to end. I'm going to Key West, and then I head back home, turn in the camper, and start booking trips for my clients again. But writing in my blog is my number one priority because of my sponsors and advertisers. I love taking those free trips! I even had a thought the other night about writing a book about this adventure. But I'm putting that on the back burner till I get home. Have to make sure I have things to write about first," Kate said.

"I think you are off to a very good beginning. Vampires, bats, spiders. And dare I say bathhouses!" Brandon said as he chuckled at the comment.

"You know, you're right. I do know that it might be difficult going back to a desk after having all this time to myself and no one dictating my schedule."

"Are you kidding? You might have time to yourself but your readers are practically telling you where you should go, what to do, and how long to stay."

"How do you know?" Kate asked.

"Because I've been reading your blog," Brandon said casually. "It seems you're quite popular. I think you could even design your own app. Center it all around your travels. There has to be a hook in there somewhere."

"My very own app. That would be kinda cool!"

Kate loved the casual talk at dinner. It felt so right. The atmosphere. The man. And now the food was before them, and it smelled so good.

"I think I filled up on chips and salsa! But this all smells so delicious," Kate said as the aromas of the food swirled around her and it didn't matter that she was almost full. She would eat what she could and get a to-go box for the rest. It would be a snack or dinner tomorrow. "Oh, this is so good. I'm so glad you suggested coming here," Kate said with her mouth practically full.

"I'm glad you approve. This has always been one of my favorite places to eat though most of the restaurants around here are great," Brandon said.

They finished their dinners and traded stories about everything: childhood, work, traveling, and more. As they sat there, Brandon knew for sure he was falling in love with the woman sitting across the table from him. She was amazing in every way, and knowing more about her life just made her more enticing.

"Are we still on for an evening swim when we get back to the campground?" Brandon asked.

"I'm looking forward to it. Does it still sound good to you?"

"Most definitely!" he said. Looking at Kate, he watched a bit of red splash across her cheeks.

They walked to the van to head back to the campers. The heat of the day had dissipated slightly, but it was still warm outside. It was perfect for an evening in the water, and when Kate looked above, the sky was cloudless. She couldn't wait to hopefully be alone with Brandon while swimming under the stars. Since it was late, she hoped the pool would be all theirs—even if they had to sneak in.

* * *

"Are you ready?"

Kate heard Brandon's voice outside her RV. She had brought several swimsuits with her, and she couldn't decide which one to choose. Finally she went with the purple and turquoise two-piece bikini. She grabbed her cover-up and towel and headed out the door.

The sight that greeted her had her weak in the knees. Even though she could only see him from the glow of the porch light on the camper, she could still make out little details. Brandon was standing before her, and he was shirtless with dark-aqua swim trunks on. What captured her attention were his six-pack abs. Brandon looked as if he worked out every day, but she had never seen him exercise once since they had been traveling together. She had already noticed his strong arms and what she deemed his nearly perfect physique, but to see so much of him had her at a loss for words.

"I think the pool is closed, but we'll hop over the fence. It's pretty short, and I can help you," he said.

Kate comprehended what Brandon had said but could only nod in agreement as they walked toward the pool. She was still under his spell. "I also commandeered Ian's and Dana's floats. At first, Ian wanted to come with us, but Missy told him no way and winked at me. Think maybe she's helping us have some date time."

Kate had to laugh a little. She could just imagine what was going on in Missy's mind, and she knew it wouldn't be long before Laurie would know the whole story too. "Knowing Missy, even this short time, I'm positive she was helping us have some time alone."

They reached the pool, and the gate was locked as Brandon had thought. After a quick hop over the fence, though, they had the swimming area all to themselves. He glanced over and watched as Kate took off her cover-up. Though the light around them was very faint, he could see the shape of her body. Every curve from her delicate neck, her slender waist down to her shapely legs was in view. He had imagined the scene before him many times, but to finally witness it in person was true pleasure.

"It's so dark," Kate said, and she finally reached the steps that went down into the dark pool.

"I'm right behind you," Brandon said, and he put his hand on her shoulder.

"The water feels fantastic. Warm but not hot. Just right for a summer night. It still feels kinda scary, though, because I can't see where I'm swimming."

Just then, Kate felt a pair of gentle yet strong arms embrace her waist from behind, and she turned around to face the sexy man holding her.

"Hi there! And you don't have to worry about that. I'm here with you." Brandon spoke in a husky voice that was almost a whisper.

They were so close, and they finally closed the small gap between them. Then their lips touched, and though they were in the pool, it was as if a wildfire had spread between them. Brandon couldn't get enough of Kate, and Kate couldn't get enough of him. She wrapped her arms around his neck and slid her hands through his hair. His hands wandered gently from her waist up her back. He moved so slowly that it gave Kate goose bumps even though they were in the warm water. One kiss after another sent waves of pleasure through both of them.

"I've been waiting for that all day," Brandon said as they both came up for air, even though neither had been under the water yet.

"I wished you hadn't waited," Kate said softly. "Brandon, I know I might sound a bit forward, but I really like you. I know we're from completely different parts of the country and might never see each other again once this is over, but I hope we do. You're like no other man I've ever dated. You're a gentleman. You're funny, even if you do have a tendency to tease me. I was always told as a little girl that if a boy picked on you it was because he liked you. You're sweet and kind to everyone and…" She cleared her throat. "Very handsome. What more could a girl ask for?"

There. Kate had laid out her feelings. As soon as the words were out of her mouth, she felt so self-conscious but glad that she had let Brandon finally know her true feelings toward him.

"Then I guess great minds think alike," Brandon said. He continued to hold her tightly yet gently in the waters of the darkened swimming pool. "You have to know how much I like you, Kate. You're brilliant, funny, and talented. Being with you makes me smile, and I find myself thinking about you all the time. And you're completely adorable and very sexy to top off everything."

With those last words, his mouth found hers once again, and they continued to move slowly through the swimming pool.

"Where are the floats you brought?" Kate said suddenly.

"Right over there. Why?"

"Let's do some water stargazing."

"Think we could fit on just one float?" Brandon said, giving her a wink.

"Let's try."

It took a few times, but Kate and Brandon were soon lying together on one float. Their arms and legs were entangled as they were gazing above at the beautiful night sky.

"It's amazing how clear the sky is and how many stars you can see tonight," she said. As she stared up at the clear night sky, she smiled as happiness radiated from her as she cuddled on the float in the warm water with this loving man.

"If you think is great, wait till you're at Bryce Canyon. You just have to camp there. You're at an elevation of about eight thousand feet, and with no lights around, the view is spectacular. I have to agree with you, though. This is pretty nice—and not just because of the stars," he said and gave her a quick kiss on the forehead.

"Did you hear that?" Kate said quickly. She thought she heard a rumble of thunder in the distance.

"Yeah, but I don't see a cloud in the sky."

As they both turned toward the direction of the sound, their once stable float gave way and they tumbled into the water. They came up laughing but was greeted with another bit of thunder and this time it was louder.

"I guess we need to head back to the campers. I've lived here my whole life and these little storms can come up quite fast."

"But I'm not ready to go," Kate said with a pout, keeping her arms wrapped around him. Then a flash of lightning lit up the sky. "OK, now I'm ready."

In what seemed a split second, Kate was up the steps and putting on her cover-up.

"Wow, you move fast!"

"I've always been scared of lightning. When I was a teenager, one of our neighbors got struck once, and it was terrifying. All of us kids learned a big lesson that day," Kate said.

She was ready to go by the time Brandon was up on the side of the pool. They grabbed the floats and headed back to the camper. They dropped the floats off at the Tates' travel trailer, making sure they were secure for the upcoming storm.

"Come on in," Kate said, and she unlocked the camper door. "As a matter of fact, since it's about to storm, why don't you stay the night in the motor home instead of your tent? I have plenty of places to sleep. You can have the bed in the front."

Brandon looked at her and wondered if he should give in to this idea. He would love to spend the night with her—not like she had suggested—but being in the camper with her would be a treat. Plus it would be nice to sleep in a bed instead of on the inflatable mattress he had been using. A bit of air conditioning during the warm night would also be nice.

"Well? I promise I'll be a good girl," Kate said with a wicked smile on her face.

"Since you made a promise, I guess I'll take you up on the offer. But you know everyone is going to be talking in the morning," Brandon warned her.

"I don't care. It will definitely give Laurie and Missy something to chew on," Kate giggled.

"Let me go get some of my things, and I'll be right back."

"I'm going to take a quick shower, but I'll leave the door unlocked."

At the thought of Kate taking a shower, Brandon's mind began playing tricks on him. Keep yourself composed, he told himself, but the thoughts of her with water dripping down her body kept coming to him no matter what he did.

When he got back with his laptop, clothes, and a few personal items, Kate had made up the bed in the front of the motor home, and he could hear the shower water running. He put his things down and set up his laptop on the dining table. He needed to write a few e-mails before going to bed, but since their nighttime swim had been interrupted by the thunderstorm, he was hoping that they could continue their date by watching a movie on television.

"Do you want to take a shower? I have extra towels."

Brandon looked up to see Kate standing with a big, fluffy towel wrapped around her body. Her wet hair clung to her shoulders. She was beautiful, and if he had anything to say or do about it, she was going to be his. "Sure. You don't mind?"

"I wouldn't have offered if I did, silly. The towels are in the bathroom. It's like showering in a closet, but I'm used to it by now. Have to say, the bathhouse has spoiled me as far as the room it gives you, and I would be there now if not for the storm outside."

Storming it was. The heavy rain sounded soothing on the roof above, and Kate thought it was so romantic. As Brandon took his shower, she put on her comfy pajamas. She avoided anything overly sexy and went with a pair of shorts and a T-shirt. She toweled off her hair and sat at the dining table. She noticed Brandon had left his laptop open. It was hard not to notice he was in his e-mail account, so she went to close the lid. Just as she reached her hand toward the device, she felt her body go numb. She recognized the name of the e-mail recipient and knew the address immediately. Kate couldn't help but read the letter—even though she knew it was an invasion of Brandon's privacy. It was personal now.

Mr. Palmer,

Kate is still doing great. Her skills driving the motor home seem to be improving. She can set up the RV quickly now. We did have a run-in with a rattlesnake today, but she is fine. I'll keep you updated, but she is doing terrific. I'll write again soon. Have a nice evening!

Brandon

Why was Brandon e-mailing her father about her? How did he even know her father? Kate felt so confused as she sat back against the cushioned seat. What exactly was going on?

Twenty-Two

The bathroom was small, but the hot water felt good. Brandon inhaled deeply, the smell of Kate still lingering in the room. He couldn't forget the way she felt in his arms while they floated in the pool. The feelings that were growing for this woman was like nothing Brandon had experienced before. He had thought he loved someone once long ago, but that had been nothing compared to what he was feeling for Kate. He couldn't utter those three little words just yet to her but there was no doubt that he was falling in love with this dazzling girl.

Brandon got dressed and stepped out of the bathroom. As he looked for Kate, he found her sitting at the dining table. His laptop was in front of her. Suddenly, a feeling of dread enveloped him. She was sitting so still. Her back was to him, and he could see he had left the browser open to his e-mails with the one he had written to Kate's father opened where she could easily read it. Oh shit!

Kate could feel Brandon standing behind her. She was still trying to process everything and didn't dare turn to look at him. "Just tell me why, Brandon. I know I shouldn't have read your e-mails. I was only getting ready to shut the laptop when I saw my father's name. Why? How do you know him? Are you babysitting me, or is it something else? Was everything you told me a lie? Everything we have done together just an act?" Kate was still facing away from him, but he heard her loud and clear. The hurt in her voice was unmistakable.

Brandon walked slowly to the table and sat across from her. He wanted to choose his words carefully because he loved this girl. His heart was suddenly telling him he might have just made the biggest mistake of his life not telling her his secret before now.

"Kate, please, before you say anything, let me tell you the whole story. Can you promise me that? Please?" Brandon held his breath and waited for her answer.

"OK." The word that came from Kate was said with no feeling, and Brandon felt as if a thick layer of ice had just settled in the RV.

"I already told you about how my dad and I had a huge disagreement and I left town to just get away from everything. I knew I could work from my laptop, and I essentially went home, packed what I needed, and made a few arrangements to make sure my house was taken care of. I really didn't even say good-bye to my father.

"I hit the road. I wanted to travel east, to get as far away from Arizona as I could. I had been on the road about three weeks when I received a call from my dad. At first, I wasn't going to pick it up, but for some odd reason, I decided to. We finally talked about everything that happened, and he apologized. When he asked when I was coming home, I told him I didn't know. I still needed time to myself. He asked if I could do him a favor, and he said he was willing to pay me.

"See, my dad is new to Facebook, and an old friend from college friended him. They used to be roommates at school. Anyway, they called each other and spent a lot of time talking. During the conversation, apparently the man told my dad that his daughter was taking a cross-country trip by herself in a motor home. Something she had never done before. He was worried but didn't want her to know. My dad told yours that I was out traveling and a little bit about why I had left. When they found out how close I was to you, your dad wondered if I might be able to find you. So he told me that you just left that morning and was heading to Biloxi, Mississippi." Brandon paused as he looked over at Kate. She was staring out the window at the pouring rain. "Your dad just wanted to make sure you were safe.

"At first, I told my Dad no because you were heading west, the complete opposite of where I wanted to go. Then I saw you at the campground."

"You saw me in Biloxi? How did you know it was me?" Kate's voice was still cold but soft.

"Your father sent me a picture and gave me a description of your motor home. He asked me to keep my distance, but if you had any problems, he wanted me to let him know. Or help you out if I could. I knew it would be tricky. If you always saw my van where you were staying, you might think you had a stalker on your hands. So, I decided that if I was going to do this, I wanted to meet you. But it's not what you're thinking," Brandon said.

"And what am I thinking?" Kate sounded angry now, and Brandon couldn't blame her.

He had wanted to tell her about the arrangement her father had requested from the moment they had met in Mississippi but could never figure out how because each moment he spent with her, he had been falling for her a bit more. But he knew keeping secrets, however, wasn't the best way to start a friendship—or relationship.

"I'm not really sure. But, Kate, I have to tell you something, and I'm being totally honest."

"Are you sure you can handle that?" Kate spat the words at him.

"I promise. I wasn't keen on this idea at first, but when I saw you, I was intrigued. Then, when we went on that vampire tour in New Orleans, I was hooked. On you. I couldn't quit thinking about you and that had me in a place where I felt confused. That's when I decided I was going to call this whole thing off and just go on to Galveston. I had been taking this trip to clear my head and try to get some semblance of my former life back. They had a beach, even if it wasn't Florida. But I found my thoughts always wondering back to you, Kate. Even as I drove south and away from you. That's why I ended up in San Antonio. I knew I had to find you again and I've followed you ever since. Not because I had to but because I wanted to."

Kate sat still. She was still staring out the window. She didn't know what to think. The whole situation was making her head swirl with such mixed emotions. Should I be mad? she thought. If so, at whom? Dad? Brandon? Both? "What about all those things you said to me? How you wanted to be with me. How I was special. Were those all lies just to keep me on the hook? So you could continue to follow me around?"

"I'd say them again because I mean them with all my heart. I want to be here. I want to be with you! I think I'm falling in love with you, Kate. No. I know I am." Brandon couldn't believe he just spoke those words out loud. This was not how he wanted to tell her. "Please believe me. All this has taken me by surprise, but I still felt I should let your Dad know you were safe, happy, and having a good time. He has been so worried about you, even though, and these were his words, you are the most capable woman he has ever known, and he's proud to call you his daughter." Brandon continued to look at her, but she only stared out the window. The rain was now coming to an end.

"Brandon, I hate to do this to you, but I think you should go. I need time to think. I can't even call my dad tonight like I wanted to. I'm afraid of what I might say."

Kate's nerves were shot. What had been such a magical evening only minutes before was suddenly a mangled mess. She wanted so badly to tell this man across from her that she believed every single word he spoke. She also wanted to return with her own declaration of the feelings she had for him. But she couldn't right now. He had kept a big secret from her, and now what trust they had between them was gone. With the word "trust" floating in her head, it made her think of Thomas and the charade he had pulled on her in San Antonio and his startling revelations. She was beginning to wonder if she was just meant to be alone in this world.

Brandon packed up his few things, including the dreaded laptop, and he slowly made his way to the door. "Kate, please look at me."

Kate didn't want to because she feared her resolve to make him leave would melt but she turned her head slowly to look at

Brandon. Her emotions were raw, and seeing him made her hurt so badly inside. *Why did he keep such a big secret from me?*

"Please think about what I've said. I mean this with every fiber of my being—I want to be with you. Only you. Because I truly love you."

Then Brandon walked out of the door. Kate quickly got up, locked it, and closed all the shades. She couldn't get in bed fast enough. She grabbed her tablet and crawled under the covers. She tried to distract herself with reading and even a game of solitaire, but suddenly the tears she had been holding back began to flow in earnest. Up to that point, the day and evening had been as close to perfect as possible between the two of them. As she wiped away the tears, she had an idea, and she did some investigating on her tablet. She suddenly knew what she had to do.

* * *

"Where is she?" Brandon asked when he arrived at Kate's camp spot early the next morning. He was looking at the small family sitting at their picnic table, enjoying their morning breakfast cereal.

"You talking about the RV that was there last night?"

Brandon was a bit frantic now, but he tried to sound calm. "Yes. Did you see her leave?"

"Yeah. She left around six o'clock this morning. As a matter of fact, she was causing all kinds of racket and woke me up. Really surprised she didn't wake up the whole campground. It sounded as if she was tearing up her campsite." The man speaking didn't sound upset. He was just very matter of fact.

Brandon, though, could just envision Kate leaving in a very angry state. His next step was to go tell Richard and Laurie what was going on. This was something he hated to do because he could just imagine what they might think about him and the entire situation. He had made a mess of things but he had to make it right. He had to find Kate.

"You mean you've been spying on her? Her daddy didn't think she was capable because she was a woman? Goodness, that girl has traveled the world. I think she can handle a motor home." Laurie definitely wasn't her cheery self this morning after Brandon sat down and told them the entire story. Well, almost all of it.

"Honey, you can't tell me that if Kate was one of our girls, you and I might not have done the same thing," Richard said.

"It started out like an assignment, but…" Brandon trailed off.

"But what?" Richard said.

"After I met her, I wanted to be with her. Now I don't know where she's gone. I dread calling her father—and mine too. They thought I was keeping a nice distance. I haven't told either one we were actually becoming friends and maybe more." Brandon looked down at his hands. He didn't want to see the looks on Richard's or Laurie's faces. He was also worried.

"Did she give you any indication where she was headed next?" Laurie said.

"We talked yesterday, but everyone was either staying here for a couple of days or not sure of the next destination. Kate does have reservations at the campground at the Grand Canyon but not for a few more days."

"Have you tried calling her?" Richard asked.

"That's a dumb question," Laurie shot back to her husband. "Can't you see this poor boy is a bit frantic? That's the first thing in the world he would do. Right?" she said, looking at Brandon as if he better answer yes.

"Of course I did! She has at least ten missed calls and messages from me. I tried to explain, like I did last night, but she isn't answering."

"Then you head to the Grand Canyon. If she has reservations, she'll show up. Plus, she has come a long way. She drives the camper well. Knows just about how everything works. Still a little prissy about getting her hands dirty, but that's just the woman in her." With that statement, Richard received a smack on the arm from his wife. "Just kidding, trying to lighten the situation a bit."

"Well, this is serious. Feels like Kate is a daughter and now I'm worried," Laurie said.

"Did you guys decide what you're going to do?" Brandon asked, even though he just wanted to get on the road.

"We're going to visit with Liz's friend for a couple of days and then head to Las Vegas. Going to stay there for a week. Hate to break up our little caravan, but I was hoping we could all meet in Vegas. Was going to ask everyone this morning. The Tates were talking about going on to California, so I'll find out a little later today. Right now, I think you better call some dads and then get on the road. Go find your girl!" Richard smiled at Brandon to give him encouragement. It was exactly what he needed.

"Brandon, you didn't exactly handle this very well, but I have a good feeling about you and Kate," Laurie said. "Just give her some space and time. It will work out. I just know we'll see you two lovebirds again."

Laurie came around the table and gave Brandon a hug before he rushed off to his van. He packed as quickly as he could. He had to find Kate and make this right.

Twenty-Three

Despite not sleeping much, Kate felt energized as she drove Interstate 17 north through Arizona. She was heading toward the Grand Canyon and basically running on adrenaline from everything that had happened the night before. She called the campground at the canyon first thing that morning and was able to secure extra nights. Now, she would spend almost a week there, which was fine with her. There were many things to do, and she was already going to the bottom of the canyon on the mule ride. That included an overnight stay at Phantom Ranch by the Colorado River. She was lucky enough to get a reservation. When she made the decision to do this ride, it was mainly because, once again, so many of her readers had insisted she would love it. At the time, Kate had been excited but very scared.

Now, the thought of traveling to the bottom of the enormous canyon soothed her. Even though she had a slight fear of heights and the thought of riding on a mule wasn't appealing, going on the ride felt very important to her. She wanted to prove that she was capable of taking care of herself. Of making good decisions. That she was a strong woman. After Brandon's revelation last night that he had basically been on "babysitting duty" traveling with her, she felt this overwhelming need to prove herself. What disappointed her was that she had been feeling more confident each day about this trip that she had been so reluctant to take. And all it took was this one incident and she felt completely deflated. She just needed this time, as she was driving to the canyon and the extra camping time there, to enjoy the beauty around her and contemplate what had happened last night.

As she continued to drive, thoughts of Brandon filled her mind. If he had only told her what was going on between him and her father. Then again, would she have understood? Would everything have been okay? She couldn't answer her own question. Then his words of love also pressed in on her. They had only known each other for a short time, but she felt the same way too. But now the trust was gone. Why do the men in my life do that? Am I at fault? At that thought, Kate sat up straighter and yelled into the air, "Hell no!" I didn't do a damn thing wrong, she thought to herself. Absolutely nothing!

As more time passed and she was coming to grips with the situation, she had to admit that she had two men in her life that really cared for her: her father and Brandon. She instantly felt grateful and lucky but the hurt of not being told what was going on still lingered causing Kate to feel so conflicted.

It seemed as if no time had passed before she found herself in Flagstaff, Arizona. Kate filled up the gas tank of Monster, walking around and stretching a bit before she headed north to see one of the seven natural wonders of the world, the Grand Canyon. As she drove the road north, this part of Arizona seemed totally different from the south, but it was beautiful all the same. As she looked around the area, she suddenly missed her camping caravan family and wished she hadn't departed so quickly. Kate felt totally alone, but at the same time, she realized that she was actually doing this by herself. She packed this morning, readied the RV for travel and was almost at her destination. Even amid the emotional turmoil in her mind, she felt a smile coming. She had to write another blog post tonight, and once again, she thought she just might have to thank Bubba for making such a bold statement that fateful day not so long ago.

As she turned left onto the main road, it was now going to be a two-lane stretch of highway up to the canyon. This would be a first for her since leaving home, but she could feel the canyon calling to her, and she needed some quiet time to sort things out.

* * *

*I*t hadn't taken long for Brandon to pack up and be on the road after talking to the Maddens. He knew he couldn't be that far behind Kate. Maybe just a couple of hours. Would she stop along the way? If so, where? Sedona? Flagstaff? Would she go straight to the canyon? He placed a bet she would head to the destination they had talked so much about just the night before. So that was where he was going. If she didn't show up for a few days, he would just wait. He had called ahead to the campground, and they only had tent spaces left, which was perfect for him.

Brandon had also placed the feared call to Kate's father, and he couldn't believe he wasn't upset. As a matter of fact, Martin Palmer just said he had wondered how long it would take before

Kate figured it all out. He assured Brandon she would be OK. She just needed to settle down and have time to think about it. Then he asked Brandon a question that startled him: What are your intentions toward my daughter?

At first, Brandon didn't know what to say because he never thought the older man would ask such a question. Brandon was honest, though. He told Martin he was in love with Kate. Brandon waited for her father to give him warnings and tell him to leave Kate alone, but instead what he heard on the other end of the line was laughing.

"Well, I never saw that coming," Martin said into the phone.

"What, sir?" Brandon said.

"That my daughter would take a big solo trip for starters. Then meet someone she loves along the way."

Wait a minute—what did he say? "How do you know she loves me?" Brandon asked.

"She hasn't said it outright, but she has talked about a 'friend' who has been a big help. The tone of her voice told me volumes. I haven't heard that type of excitement in her voice in a long time. Even though she did try to act as though it wasn't a big deal. I can read my daughter like a book, even through a telephone conversation. But you also answered another question for me. I tried calling her last night and this morning. Couldn't figure out why she didn't answer, and now I know the full story. I guess she'll call when she feels up to it. Though, I hope it's sooner rather than later."

"Me too," Brandon said. "I plan on going on to the canyon and waiting for her there. We were just talking about her next stop last night while floating in the pool—" Brandon stopped himself before giving out too much information.

"Son, all I ask is you don't break her heart. I would ask you to stay away since she just got out of a relationship with that idiot, Thomas, who's been begging me to talk to Kate for him but I finally told him it was over and to leave her and me alone. There really never was a connection between those two. But I can tell, just through telephone conversations with her, you and your e-mails that there is something special between the two of you. Just be good to her."

"I promise," Brandon said. He smiled and released a big sigh. "As soon as I find her, I will let you know. Thanks, Mr. Palmer."

"Call me Martin."

* * *

*A*s soon as Kate saw the entrance to the national park, she breathed a huge sigh of relief. The road between Flagstaff and the park wasn't bad, but it had challenged her RV driving skills. There were many inclines, twists, and turns. Going around a mountain, all on a two-lane road, had her knuckles white yet again as she gripped the steering wheel tight like before when she was in anxious situations. Though the scenery was beautiful as she drove, she found herself a little too edgy as to enjoy her surroundings completely. And she had more than her fair share of motorists go around her. She followed the park signs to the campground, but as she made a turn, she could see a small glimpse of the mighty Grand Canyon. Her breath caught in her throat at the tiny bit she saw. Suddenly, all the turmoil from last night and today seemed to fade, if only for a little while. She couldn't wait to get a closer look. Just get the RV set up and then walk to the rim, she thought. After that, she could just sit, soak in the beauty, and give herself even more time for contemplation.

Kate checked in to the campground and found her space. She was once again thankful she could pull through. This time, she didn't have her friends to help. By now, though, she was sure she'd make new ones as her travels continued to take her around the United States. Still, she missed Richard, Laurie, and Liz, who would probably be upset she missed her latest crochet lesson, but Kate told herself she would keep up with the craft now that she knew what she was doing. And that she was able to tuck away the memory of her mother's leaving her so long ago. She also didn't get a chance to tell the Tates good-bye and would miss the antics of their two children. But most of all, she was missing Brandon, and the more hours that passed, the deeper that pain felt.

Part of her wanted to call him, tell him where she was, and hope he would come be with her. Part of her wanted to tell him it was OK and that she could forgive him. There was also the part of her that was scared to let this incident go, afraid of putting herself in a vulnerable position again. What if there were other secrets waiting to be told? She didn't want a broken heart, but then again, she really had never felt like this for another man. What she felt for Brandon was completely different from the jumble of emotions she had experienced in any relationship until him.

Kate was getting so good at setting up the motor home by now that it didn't take her long to have everything up and connected. As soon as she was finished, she quickly grabbed her tote bag and filled it with a drink, some snacks, a notepad, pen, her phone, and her nice digital camera. She was going to see the canyon in all its glory for the first time, and by the looks of it, sunset wasn't too far away.

Kate followed the signs to the canyon's rim. When she got near the Bright Angel Lodge, people were milling about, but she could see the edges of the canyon. As she got closer and closer, her heart beat faster. Of all the places she and her dad had talked about her visiting, this was tied for first place with a few other notable spots. She had seen it once, as she flew over it and couldn't believe how grand it was then. Now, to be right at the edge was completely different.

"Are you excited?"

The voice she heard coming from behind her was familiar and brought a wave of excitement and tears. It was him. Brandon had found her. How should I react? she quickly wondered.

Kate's mind was so jumbled and torn between ignoring him and continuing to head to the edge of the canyon or turning around and running into his arms. She still was upset over the previous night's events, but she couldn't help herself. She turned to see him. He was a sight for sore eyes. He looked ruggedly handsome as he stood there and waited for her to respond to his question.

Kate began slowly walking to him. Her eyes were steady on him, and she didn't see the small ledge she had stepped over only a few minutes ago. She felt herself and her bag go flying in the air, but once again, Brandon was there to catch her in the nick of time and kept her from falling into the gravel. His balance wasn't the best this time, however, and they both tumbled to the rocks. Brandon took the brunt of the fall.

"Are you all right?" Kate said quickly. She tried to look him over for any for scrapes, cuts, or even broken bones. He had, after all, broken her fall.

"I'm perfectly fine now that I'm with you," Brandon said, even though his arm was stinging, and he could feel the small rocks on his back.

But having her in his arms took away all that pain. He reached up and gave her a gentle kiss, which Kate eagerly returned. She realized then that her body was betraying her mind.

"I'm still mad at you," Kate said, but the words weren't as harsh as the night before.

"You have every right to be," Brandon said, as they both got up.

They looked around to see they had a small audience. The people just smiled as the two got up from their very romantic position on the ground.

"I think I understand why you didn't say anything. Mainly because I know my dad. He wants me to be independent, but he is concerned about me too. I still think you should have told me, though. How do I know I can trust you now?"

"I guess the only thing I can do is to prove it through my actions. You know everything now."

"I really know everything?"

"Everything. You can trust me, Kate. I promise. I'll give you character references if I have to. Just let me prove it to you. I even talked to your dad today. He told me he was surprised you hadn't found out about all this before now."

"You talked to my Dad?"

"Yeah, I had to let him know what had happened. He said he was wondering why you weren't answering any of his calls. He didn't know what had happened between you and me, and he just wanted me to tell him you were OK. I couldn't, though, because you took off this morning like a bat out of hell," Brandon said. He now sounded a little irritated with her.

"Do you blame me? How would you feel if you were in my position?"

This reunion was not going like Brandon had planned. He tried to stay calm and explain again, but Kate didn't give him a chance. "Brandon, I just need more time to myself so I can think about everything that has happened. But right now I'm going to go see my very first view of the canyon, and I want to do it by myself. Tomorrow, I'm going on the mule ride to the bottom of the canyon, and I'm staying at the Phantom Lodge overnight. When I get back, let's talk then. OK?" Kate was trying to remain calm. She knew she needed some time, but her heart wanted him to experience everything with her.

"No problem. I understand. You know how to find me. VW van with a tent. I'll be waiting, Kate."

With that, Brandon turned around and started walking back to the campground. She watched only for a few seconds, and tears returned to her eyes. She then made her way to a viewing spot her readers had suggested.

As Kate stood and looked at the sight before her, she was in such awe. Now she didn't know if the tears in her eyes were from seeing Brandon or the incredible sight before her. There were no words. The Grand Canyon was just that: grand and majestic. She almost felt as if she was looking at some kind of illusion or picture. It was simply hard to believe what she was seeing. She suddenly wished she had someone to share this wonderful moment with and turned around just to see if Brandon still might be there but he was gone. She knew all she had to do was call him, and he would probably join her, but she couldn't bring herself to make the phone call. So, she sat on the ledge and looked out at the vastness of the canyon. Down below her were several very healthy looking squirrels that tourists definitely fed, and she watched them scamper back and forth. She observed the families, couples, and individuals all taking in the beauty before them.

Kate suddenly remembered Bubba's comment that had sent her on this journey: "You like traveling to all these fancy places, flying first class and staying in five-star hotels. But what about those of us who can't come and go like that? Why don't you try something simpler like camping? You would get to see some great places. Bet you can't do it." She couldn't say camping had been simpler but the travel lifestyle it offered was satisfying. She was glad she had accepted Bubba's challenge.

As Kate reflected on her trip so far, the sights and things she had experienced weren't available by flying over them. Or taking a train that whizzed by. It was traveling on the road and stopping when you saw something that piqued your interest. It was meeting people like Henry and Jean in Biloxi who invited her to her first RV dinner. It was vampire tours, riverboat rides, snakes, tarantulas, bat flights, and more. The more Kate thought about it, the more she realized all she had yet to see on this camping trip of hers. Though, in complete honesty, she was still looking forward to some hotel time in Vegas, but she finally understood what was so special about traveling in an RV.

Kate watched the sunset, taking picture after picture. As she continued to sit on the ledge, she finally decided to call her father.

"Hi there, kiddo. Are you pissed at your pop?" Martin said when he answered the phone.

"Yes and no," Kate responded. "I know your heart was in the right place. I just wish you had a bit more faith in me."

"Kate, I have more faith in you than you'll ever know. You are smart, witty, and beautiful—inside and out. I know you are more than capable to make this trip all on your own, but I'm just being a dad. And dads worry about their little girls, even if they are grown."

At those words, Kate could no longer be upset with her father. Tears came to her eyes as she talked to him. She also looked over the beautiful sight before her.

"So, where are you exactly so I can quit worrying?" her father said.

"Brandon didn't call you with my whereabouts?" Kate said, with a bit of sarcasm mixed with a slight laugh."

"I haven't heard from him since this morning. Have you?"

"I'm at the Grand Canyon. I'm actually sitting on the rim and watching the last bit of a sunset. It's beautiful, Dad, and I wish you were here with me," Kate said wistfully.

"I wish I was there too. I've only seen the canyon once, and it was wonderful. But you didn't answer my question. Have you heard from Brandon?" her father asked once more.

"He found me, and we had a run-in. Literally." Kate gave her dad the details of the two tripping and landing in the gravel in a tangled heap. She could hear him chuckle.

"Well, what did he say?"

"Why?" Kate said. She wondered about her father's sudden interest.

"Just making sure the boy's fine. When I talked to him this morning, he was a bit frantic because he couldn't find you."

"Frantic? Probably ashamed or guilty about all this spying on me."

"Listen, if you want to blame anyone, blame me. Brandon just agreed to help me out and found more than he bargained for."

"What do you mean by that?" Kate said.

"Brandon told me how he feels about you. And from the way you talk about him, I think the feeling is mutual. So don't hold on to this frustration and anger too long. It's not good for either of you. But, I just hope you'll forgive your old man," Martin said.

"I do, Dad. And I love you. I'll talk to you in a few days. I'm taking the mule ride down into the canyon and spending the night. I'll call when I get back."

"Wow! When we talked about that, I really didn't think you would go. Proud of you! Have a blast and I love you too, baby girl."

With that, Kate's father clicked the disconnect button.

Twenty-Four

There wasn't much for Kate to get ready the next morning before leaving for her mule ride. She could only bring a few things with her. Everything else would be provided for the tour group members at the lodge at the bottom of the canyon. As the time got closer for her to get on the mule and ride to the Phantom Ranch below, her anxiety level progressed higher, but she kept it in check by deep breathing and pep talks. If only Brandon was going, everything would be OK, she thought. Then Kate would think about how capable she was for doing this on her own, and she remembered the tender words her dad had told her last night.

As she approached the group, she suddenly felt anxious, not knowing anyone. Kate knew she needed this alone time, even though the thought of sheer cliffs terrified her, and this would be her first experience riding on a large animal. She checked in and went to listen to the instructions. She concentrated so intently, wanting to make sure she didn't deviate from anything the guide said. The more he talked, the more nervous she became. Maybe I should just cancel this whole thing, Kate thought as the anxiety rose up inside her once again.

"I was wondering when you were going to show up."

The voice came from behind her yet again. Kate turned around to see Brandon standing there with a small pack in his hands.

"What are you doing here?" she asked. She wanted to sound annoyed, but secretly she had never been so happy to see a familiar face—especially his face.

"After I talked to you last night, I came to see if there were any spots left for the ride down to the ranch. I got lucky because someone made other plans, and I was able to claim the spot," Brandon said with a smile.

"They had other plans?" Kate asked. She had a sneaking suspicion that wasn't the true story. "Want to tell me the truth this time?"

"I am!" Brandon exclaimed. "I just kinda helped those 'plans' along. I paid for someone's spot. His friends protested, but he preferred the money to heights. There is just one problem."

"What might that be?" Kate eyed him and tried her best not to smile.

"We might have to share a cabin at the ranch below. I told the gentleman I didn't think it would be an issue since we knew each other. We did almost spend the other night together anyway."

"Before you lied to me."

"Kate, I didn't lie to you. I just kept something from you. I didn't do it to be mean or malicious. It was two people caring for your well-being."

"Two people?"

"Yes, there are two of us." The entire time Brandon had been talking, he had been inching closer and closer to her. His voice was getting huskier and sexier with each movement. "I love you, Kate." Before she could even respond, Brandon gently placed his hand on her face and kissed her so sweetly. Kate felt as if she was in another world and the leftover hurt and frustration with this man was slipping away.

"That's the way to do it, brother!" shouted a man in the distance.

Both Kate and Brandon looked around and saw a group of guys watching them. They were clapping and cheering. Brandon gave them a thumbs-up, and Kate's cheeks were red once again.

"They were in on this?" Kate said, a slight smile graced her face.

"I kinda told them what was going on but not all the details. Just that I had to find a way onto this mule trip and I was willing to pay. I needed to correct a situation, and they were more than willing to help." Brandon stood there and looked into her eyes. He hoped she knew how he truly felt.

"I think I'm getting this whole situation sorted out in my head. I have to admit, I felt as if my privacy had been violated. You knew all about me, and I knew nothing about you."

"That's just it. I didn't know much about you. Only minor details. Your dad just wanted me to keep my distance and make sure you were OK. If you needed assistance, he wanted to know someone would be there to help. I remember him telling me he knew you were going to be OK, but he just needed reassurance. Believe me, at first I didn't want to do this at all. He pleaded with me, even offering me money but I turned it down. My dad even offered money too, which I gladly took but plan to give it back. I was going to be out on the road anyway. I figured I would check on you once—in Mississippi–then be on my way after I told your dad you were fine. But I followed you to New Orleans and after I met you, I couldn't stay away if I wanted to. I tried many times to take my mind off you, but you're just one special woman I can't forget. And now I don't want to." Brandon's voice had gone from apologetic to tantalizing in just a few sentences.

"If I'm being totally honest, I'm glad you decided to follow me. Now that I've had time to think about everything that happened, you're kinda hard to forget too," Kate said. She walked her fingers up his chest and ended with the palm of her hand on his cheek. Then she reached up to give him a kiss.

"It's time! Let's go everyone," the guide said loudly to the entire group assembled in front of him.

"I can do this. I can do this," Kate started whispering to herself.

"What?" Brandon asked.

"Nothing," she said quickly.

"I heard you say something. Are you OK?"

Kate didn't want him to know she was literally shaking from head to toe, but she couldn't help it. "I'm really scared," she said quietly so only he could hear.

"Of the trip down or the mules?" Brandon asked.

"Both, really. But I am determined to do this."

"Well, I'm right here. I've done this before, and it's a gorgeous ride. There are some places that are a bit, shall we say, breathtaking, but just remember to breathe. Concentrate on the beauty around you, looking out, not straight down. I'll also be on the mule right in front of you. That way, I can look back and check on you instead of you looking back if you need reassurance. You can do this."

Brandon took her into his arms, hugged her tightly, and helped her onto her mule. She watched as he easily got on his mule for the ride, and she gave him a weak smile. Then she took out her real camera this time for pictures because it had a strap she could put around her neck. This was much safer. Should she lose her grip with her cell phone, it would just fall to the canyon floor.

Before long, the mule train began its decent into the canyon via the Bright Angel Trail. After about thirty minutes, she was starting to feel at ease. Yes, the trails were narrow and the drop-offs on the sides were steep, but Kate felt safe. She felt a confidence like she had never experienced before. She snapped picture after picture and even took some video. There was one extremely narrow turn on a small ledge that had her shaking, but Brandon's reassuring look as her mule followed the others gave her a warm feeling inside.

Even though the beauty around her was magnificent, she found herself staring at Brandon. He looked so ruggedly handsome riding the mule in front of her. He was dressed in a T-shirt and jeans that fit him nicely. Each glance back in her direction actually made her swoon a bit inside. Kate was officially in love with this man, and since he had finally opened up to her, maybe tonight she would feel ready to tell him her true feelings. She wanted to be with him, get to know him even more, and possibly share her trip with him. She didn't know the direction of their relationship, but she hoped it would be a happy one.

"The guide said this is the last rest break before we'll be at the ranch. Still doing OK?" Brandon asked Kate, brushing a wisp of hair from her face as they stood facing each other.

"Yeah, I'm doing fine. The ride has been wonderful. There have been a few times I was a little anxious but not as much as I anticipated. And I can't believe the change in temperature. It's much warmer down here," Kate said as she took another sip from her water bottle. "I did hear the ride back up is a bit scarier, though."

"Well, we will come to that tomorrow. Right now, let's just enjoy the moment," Brandon said. He wrapped both arms around her and found her lips once more.

"You sure know how to make a girl feel good," Kate said a little breathlessly.

"You're the only girl I want to share that with." He took hold of her hand, and they walked back toward their respective mules.

This time Kate climbed up by herself. Brandon just smiled at the amazing woman who he couldn't wait to be with tonight under the stars in one of the most wondrous places on earth.

It wasn't long before the mules and their riders were finally at the ranch, and everyone went to check out the rustic cabins. Kate and Brandon entered the little building. It was nice with two bunk beds, a toilet, and a sink. There was no shower. Then Kate remembered there was a central shower area, but by now that didn't faze her. Since they hadn't brought much with them, they each chose a bunk and lay down for just a minute.

"I can't believe I'm at the bottom of the Grand Canyon. I really did it," Kate said it so softly.

"I knew you could," Brandon said.

He rolled to his side and propped his head up on his hand. Kate looked so beautiful just lying there, and he wanted so badly to just go snuggle up beside her, but he had to take things slow to win back her trust, and that was what he was going to do.

"What do you say we get showers? Then it will be time for dinner. Afterward, we will go for a walk by the Colorado River."

"That sounds perfect," Kate said, and she looked over at him and smiled happily.

Twenty-Five

For Kate, the hot shower was utterly relaxing and left her feeling refreshed. And the ranch dinner they shared with their other companions on this trip was perfect. Everything was very rustic, especially to what Kate was used to but she loved it all. She found out at dinner that it was just luck that she and Brandon had a cabin to themselves. Or was it luck? Kate didn't ask because she didn't care. Brandon was with her, and that was all that mattered.

After dinner, they walked hand in hand down the trail that led to the banks of the Colorado River. The water moved swiftly by and Kate could see the power of the mighty river. It still astonished her that it was water that had created this enormous canyon.

Neither said anything as they took the bench beside the bank of the river. It wouldn't be long before sunset, and they would need to get back to the cabin before the darkness of the canyon overtook them. But as they sat there, both seemed lost in their own thoughts.

"Kate, I have something to tell you," Brandon said tentatively. "I know things these last couple of days haven't quite gone as either of us expected, but maybe that's a good thing. Now that everything is out in the open, there's something else I need to tell you." He turned to face her, seeing her eyes turn to a shade of worry. "Kate, I don't believe in coincidences. As I look back now on all that has happened, I feel that I was meant to "babysit" you, using your words there. If I hadn't agreed to check on you, I wouldn't have met you. I wouldn't have fallen in love with you." Brandon paused and took a deep breath before he continued.

"I think I fell in love with you from almost the beginning of this adventure. Every minute I'm with you it's as if I'm in this fun, magical place I don't want to leave or let go of. The other morning, when I came around the corner and saw your RV gone, my heart sank. Not because of what your dad or even mine would say, but I knew then and there I couldn't be without you. Yesterday, when I caught up with you and you just wanted to be alone, I felt as if someone punched me in the gut. I know these are all things most guys wouldn't tell a girl, but I want you to know the truth—from me—and no one else. I say that because I think your dad has an inkling we're more than just acquaintances."

Kate looked at him, admiration and love filling her completely. As she thought about her trip so far, she realized he had been with her practically every step of the way. They had had fun together and laughed. He had taught her things about camping and protected her from all kinds of creatures. Even when he made fun of her, as he called it, "city girl" ways, it didn't really bother her. Because it was him that teased her.

Kate was in love too. With this man who had laid his heart all out for her. She scooted closer—as close as she could get to him and rested her head on his shoulder. He put his arm around her and pulled her even closer to him.

"I'm sorry I ran away yesterday, but everything seemed unreal to me. When I saw that e-mail on your computer, it just sent a jolt through me. I thought I was doing such a good job with this whole camping thing—"

"You were and still are! That's just it. You don't need me."

"But I do. That's what I want to say. I started this trip with my self-imposed rule of 'no men'. I just figured it would be a good time for me to take some time for myself since I always seem to be on the go. Sounds weird since I'm on the go now, but I knew this camping thing would be different. A slower pace than the type of traveling I was used to. After the Thomas fiasco in San Antonio, I wanted really to swear off men but I had already met you. It just seemed as if everything we did was, I don't know, right. It felt good. Fun. Exciting. Being with you was—is—very enticing. I'll even admit something. When you decided to go to Galveston, I was wishing you would go to San Antonio instead. And that was before Thomas had even made an appearance on this trip!

"You make me feel so special, Brandon. Through all the experiences I've had on this camping trip so far, I'm glad I've been able to spend them with you. I can say this with no hesitation at all, and I've never been able to say this without feeling as if strings were attached, but," and Kate hesitated for only a second, "I love you. You are the guy who just gets me just the way I am. Even though I'm camping in high heels."

Those last words brought back the memory in New Orleans of her walking down that gravel camping road in high heels, her ankles wobbling and about to give way. She had learned so much since that day and a lot of it was due to Brandon. Kate stood and then proceeded to sit in Brandon's lap. She touched her forehead to his. "I really do love you, Brandon Anderson."

Those were the words he had been waiting for. Brandon reached up to touch Kate's cheek so gently, and he ran his finger along her lips. His hand caressed her back, and then he kissed her again and again. Each kiss was more fervent than the one before. He had found the woman of his dreams, and he wasn't going to let her go.

For Kate, a feeling of serenity washed over her just knowing this incredible man loved her. This man, who had given up his own trip plans to be with her. She wasn't even one-fourth of the way into her camping journey and she had found someone so special, so dear to her heart. Her mind started to think about their future and what it might hold, but she quickly pushed it aside. She wanted to be in this moment with Brandon. Just the two of them, enjoying this time with each other by the beautiful river at the bottom of the majestic canyon. It felt like a once in a lifetime moment and Kate didn't want to miss it.

When they came up for air, they both stared at each other for a few seconds and then laughed a little. They suddenly heard a round of clapping behind them again. They looked over their shoulders quickly to see some of the same guys from earlier this morning.

"Looks as if you got your girl!" a young man yelled.

"I certainly did! Thanks to you guys! If you would, please tell Gus thanks again for selling me his ticket," Brandon answered back.

"We're glad we could help out. And Gus was more than glad to take the money. You two have fun!"

Brandon looked at Kate. "Are you having fun? Is this trip what you wanted or imagined what it would be? I know you haven't traveled very far yet but what do you think up till this moment?"

Kate just smiled. "I'm definitely having fun but I can't say that it's what I expected. Yes, the challenges with the motor home are getting better. I've met some great people and made new friends. But I certainly didn't think I would have found you. I think this trip is just the beginning of something really special." She leaned into Brandon for another kiss, this time under the canopy of stars of the nighttime sky above the Grand Canyon.

"So where do we go from here?"

Epilogue

The trip back up the canyon the next morning was as beautiful as the trip they had made the day before but with a few more harrowing twists and turns. Once back at the motor home, Kate couldn't contain her excitement. She had done it! She had gone to the bottom of the Grand Canyon, spent the night at a ranch, and traveled back up. Just wait till she could blog about this, she thought. My readers are finally going to know this girl isn't all about being fancy!

But the best part of the trip was finally making a real connection with Brandon, both of them talking about their true feelings and solidifying their relationship. He loved her. She definitely hadn't expected to find that on this six-month odyssey. She would take it, though, because he was something special. And she was very much in love with him.

Back at the campground, Kate was very surprised to see Richard, Laurie, and Liz waiting on them. They had decided to follow them and camp at the canyon. They all had dinner together at the lodge that evening, and Kate and Brandon gave them the details of their trip on the mules and to the Phantom Ranch below.

"Seems as if there's more to talk about than just some mule ride," Laurie said. She was watching Kate and Brandon like a hawk and analyzing every move they made. "Seems as if you two might be a little more than just friends. Must be some magic at the bottom of this canyon," Laurie said with a smile.

Kate and Brandon looked at each other and then back to the three people sitting across from them in the restaurant. "You could definitely say that," Kate answered and rested her head on Brandon's shoulder, but not before giving him a quick kiss on the cheek.

"Thank goodness! I was wondering when this was going to happen. Especially after the story Brandon told us. Just glad you guys were able to work things out. So, where to now?"

"Kate and I have been talking, and I think she needs some hotel time. We want to head to Las Vegas for a while. Her dad and his girlfriend are flying out to meet her there. Then we'll make some short trips to Mt. Zion National Park and Bryce Canyon. Maybe even do some real camping there if Kate can handle a tent," Brandon said, giving her a wink. "They also have an awesome stargazing program. But first, are you guys game for some Vegas fun?" Brandon asked.

"Shoot, I'm always ready for Vegas," Richard said quickly.

"Me, too!" added Laurie.

"Well, that's good because Kate and I are behind on her crochet lessons. She needs to learn a few more stitches so she can make some hats and scarves before she heads up north. Doesn't matter what time of year it is. Up north, it's chilly at night. A scarf will be just whatcha need," Liz said. "Plus a nice warm body next to ya."

Everyone looked at the older lady with shock but she kept eating as though her words hadn't been anything out of the ordinary.

"Then we leave in a couple of days. Vegas it is," Kate said quickly before anything could be said about Liz's remark.

As they reached the Maddens' campsite, Laurie came and gave Kate a hug. "Remember what I told you before? He's a good man, Kate. He might not have handled this whole thing on keeping an eye on you just right but his intentions were good. Now look what has happened. Hang on tight because it's hard to find a real good man."

"Thanks, Laurie. I sure plan to. But it all depends on our travel plans. I still have a long trip ahead of me. Hopefully he will want to follow along."

"Honey, I don't think that will be any problem." Laurie gave Kate a quick hug and said goodnight.

The night was dark as Brandon and Kate walked slowly back to Kate's RV, taking their time. Their arms were wrapped around each other and in the surrounding lights emanating from the other RVs, they probably looked like one large person walking down the campground road.

"I'm going to try this again: Do you want to stay in the camper? In the front bed?" Kate asked Brandon.

"I think I better stay in my tent tonight. There's no telling what would happen if I stayed in that motor home," he said as he smiled wickedly down at her. "But we'll see about Vegas. Staying in a hotel room sounds good after all this time in a tent. I'll just make sure to get my own room."

"We'll see about that once we get there," Kate said, and she gently kissed Brandon.

"I haven't been to Vegas in quite a while. Maybe we can see a show. I've always wanted to do that."

"You have never been to a Las Vegas show? They are wonderful—well most of them are. Let's go see one of the comedy shows for sure," Kate said.

"Sounds like fun," Brandon said softly, turning her toward him. "But I can't wait to meet your Dad. Especially now," and he kissed the tip of her nose.

"I know you'll like him, and he's probably going to love you. Especially after you took care of his little girl."

"So, Vegas, here we come!" Brandon said.

"As long as I'm with you," Kate answered back with a happy smile.

Coming Soon

"Camping in High Heels : Viva Las Vegas"

*K*ate Palmer has made it to the Grand Canyon in her RV but is now in desperate need of some hotel time, if only for a few days. What better place than Las Vegas? Plus what better city to have fun in with her new boyfriend, Brandon? And she is ready to bring out her high heels for some fun out on the town.

But as things go, not all plans work out like Kate intends for them to. A visit from her father and Brandon's insistence that they visit Mt. Zion National Park and Bryce Canyon for some more camping time brings Kate back to the great outdoors and more quirky adventures.

Acknowledgments

$\mathcal{W}$ow—where do I begin? This novel was certainly a labor of love with my main inspiration coming from my wonderful parents, Sonny and Irene Slusser.

My parents worked to provide for our family by building a very successful RV business that included three thriving dealerships. During the building of the business, I was blessed to accompany my parents on many trips, mostly by motor homes and had so many adventures over the years. These wonderful times have been the inspiration Kate's story and the other novels to come. So thanks Mom and Dad—your hard work, dedication and love for the RV business brought my character, Kate Palmer, to life.

Once again, I have to thank my incredible husband, Jeff. Your love and support continue to amaze me each and every day. You do the dishes, laundry, go grocery shopping and even fix me dinner, allowing me the gift to be able to write. And you put up with me when I'm crazy involved in making a scene just right. Thank you for your unwavering belief in me. It means more than I can write in words. I love you so very much!

What can I say about my best friend/accountability partner, Donna Gauntlett? It's partly her fault that I keep writing books because last year, just through a casual conversation, the writing bug took hold and we both wrote our first books. Now, we continue on that journey but there is more to the story this time. For my new "Camping with Kate" Series, she has brought Kate's image to the cover. I could picture in my mind this wonderful girl and how I wanted to portray her on the novel cover but it was Donna's wonderful artistic skills that gave Kate her sassy style. Thanks Donna for your deep friendship and putting up with me as I kept changing my mind on colors and such! For more information on her artwork, please visit www.donnaleegauntlett.com.

To all my wonderful family that have shared your camping stories with me: Thank You! When I mentioned that I was writing this novel, your stories made me laugh and gave me food for thought on bringing the camping lifestyle to light with a little humor and love.

And to my readers: this new series is different from "The Florida Keys Romance" Series but I hope you love it just as much. It's a bit different but hopefully it will show you the fun side of camping even if you decide to wear high heels!

And to all you RVers out there: keep doing what you are doing! Camping, whether it is in a tent or a luxurious bus, is one of the best ways to see all the exciting places from large cities to small lakes to breathtaking deserts to white sandy beaches and so much more. Soaking up the great outdoors, spending time with some of the friendliest people around and relaxing in front of a campfire are simply some of the best times around.

Big Hugs to All!

Miki

***For more information about the places Kate visited in this novel, please visit my website at www.mikibennett.com for a complete list. Happy Camping!

Other Novels by Miki Bennett

*D*ivorcee Maddy Sumner is ready to work on creating the next chapter of her life. Adjusting to a newly empty nest and coping with chronic health issues, she's desperately in need of some time to rest and regroup.

So, she embarks on a much-needed vacation to the Florida Keys, with the help of her best friend Riley. There, she catches the eye of Jason, the mysterious neighbor across the street, who finds himself captivated by the beautiful woman in the rental house on the water.

When an emergency situation causes Jason and Maddy's lives to collide, it isn't long before the pair discovers meaningful feelings for one another, secured even more deeply by a whirlwind trip to Key West. But when a set of painful circumstances from the past emerges, will complications put an end to this blossoming romance?

$\mathcal{A}$ fter attending a wedding in the Keys, twenty-eight year old Abbey Wallace decides to pack up everything she owns and move to Key West. The budding artist loves the vibe of the city and hopes to become an artisan at Mallory Square.

After finding an apartment and securing a job at a web design and graphics firm, she settles into island life and begins making new friends. However, her neighbor Josie poses a challenge. Abbey persists at building a friendship, determined to find the reason behind the fifty-five year old woman's mean-spirited attitude.

Meanwhile, at work, Zach Isler soon becomes Abbey's best friend. But although he's totally enamored with her, Abbey is afraid to admit her feelings for him. Until a sudden unexpected event makes her re-examine her emotions.

Book Two in the Florida Keys Romance Series, *Forever in the Keys*, explores friendship, romance, and the excitement of life's second chances.

A handsome marine biologist comes to Key Largo and meets a beautiful and vivacious boat captain. Sounds perfect, right?

Unfortunately for Garrett Holmes and Skylar Cartwright, meeting and falling in love isn't all smooth sailing into the Florida sunset.

Despite their mutual attraction and growing feelings for one another, Skylar's rocky relationship with her wealthy parents and Garrett's jealous research assistant, Casey, make life plenty hectic for the new couple.

When Skylar's ex-boyfriend, Andrew, appears on the scene, things get really complicated, forcing Garrett and Skylar to question if love is enough to sustain them through the social storms.

An engaging and spirited romance story set against the luscious backdrop of the Florida Keys, Miki Bennett's third novel will sweep you away to a world of warm sun and emerald waters.